DESERT MEMENTOS

DESERT MEMENTOS

Stories of Iraq and Nevada

CALEB S. CAGE

UNIVERSITY OF NEVADA PRESS | *Reno & Las Vegas*

University of Nevada Press | Reno, Nevada 89557 USA
www.unpress.nevada.edu
Copyright © 2017 by University of Nevada Press
Cover photographs: (*background*) MartaJonina © iStock; (*center*) jimmyan © iStock

"The Golden Dragon" previously published in Sally Drumm's *War Stories* anthology (2012). "Ghost Patrol" previously published by Scott Yarbrough in *Forces* Journal in (2013). "Soldier's Cross" previously published in Jeffery Hess's *Home of the Brave: Somewhere in the Sand* anthology (2013). "Operation Battle Mountain" previously published by Erica Vital-Lazare in the *Red Rock Review* (2014).

"A Prayer to the Goddess" from *Things That Happen Once: New Poems* by Rodney Jones. Copyright © 1996 by Rodney Jones. Reprinted by permission of Houghton Mifflin Harcourt Publishing Company. All rights reserved.

LIBRARY OF CONGRESS CATALOGING-IN-PUBLICATION DATA
Names: Cage, Caleb S., 1979- author.
Title: Desert mementos : stories of Iraq and Nevada / Caleb S. Cage.
Other titles: Stories of Iraq and Nevada
Description: Reno : University of Nevada Press, [2017]
Identifiers: LCCN 2017025160 (print) | LCCN 2016059983 (e-book) |
    ISBN 978-1-943859-47-4 (cloth : alk. paper) | ISBN 978-0-87417-657-5
    (e-book)
Subjects: LCSH: Cage, Caleb S., 1979- | Iraq War, 2003-2011—Personal
    narratives, American. | Soldiers—United States—Biography. | United States.
    Army—Officers—Biography. | Landscape—Iraq. | Landscape—Nevada. |
    Nevada—Social life and customs. | Nevada—Biography.
Classification: LCC DS79.76 .C339 2017 (e-book) | LCC DS79.76 (print) |
    DDC 956.7044/a [B] —dc23
LC record available at https://lccn.loc.gov/2017025160

FIRST PRINTING

Manufactured in the United States of America

For Brooke: you are the happy story
you couldn't find on these pages.

```
-------------------------------------

       The Writers Block Book Shop
            1020 Fremont Street
            Las Vegas, NV 89101
               702-550-6399

     -----------Sales Receipt-----------

Trans#: 27576477
Date: 12/5/2017 7:26:19 PM
Cashier: Scott Seele       Register #: 1

Item          Description          Amount
============  ================  = ==========
9781943859474DESERT MEMENTO       $22.95
                                ==========
                    Sub Total     $22.95
                    Sales Tax      $1.89
                        Total     $24.84

     Visa/MC/Discover Tendered     $24.84
          Card: XXXXXXXXXXX5493
               Auth #: 005531
                   Change Due      $0.00
```

Contents

Acknowledgments

It goes without saying that any book is the result of the many hands that helped shape it, and this is particularly true for *Desert Mementos*. I'm someone with minimal formal training as a writer, so there were many who were crucial to this work: some who helped me write by actively mentoring me or by encouraging me through their own work, some who saw strengths in some of these stories and published them, and some whose friendship and love carried me through. What follows will be my inevitably incomplete attempt to show my sincere appreciation for all who helped make this book happen.

I would like to begin by simply thanking those I had the pleasure of serving in Iraq with in 2004: the soldiers of First Platoon, C Battery, 1-6 FA, T. J. Grider, Gregory Tomlin, John Akridge, Doug Chadwick, and too many others to name here. They brought me through the war and they brought me home. Their friendship will be with me forever.

Several writers have encouraged me along the way. Some took an interest in mentoring me directly and offered me kindness and advice: Dale Erquiaga, Cyndy Gustafson, Pinckney Benedict, Brad Summerhill, Matt Gallagher, Lea Carpenter, Todd Borg, Michael Archer, H. Lee Barnes, Don Waters, Dana Bennett, Joe McCoy, Amy Roby, Marilee Swirczek, Sharon Orsborn, Tracy Crow, Kevin Burns, Tina Drakulich, Allen Herritage, Matt Morris, and Christopher Bellavita. Others created a space and a culture for the literature of Nevada and of these wars: Willy Vlautin, Claire Vaye Watkins, Siobhan Fallon, David Abrams, Laura McBride, Brian Turner, and Christopher Coake. I am fortunate to consider many of these writers friends, and I am deeply indebted to them for their kindness.

I am grateful to several editors who included my work in the pages of their publications. Sally Drumm published what is now called "The Golden Dragon" in her *War Stories* anthology in 2012; Scott

Yarbrough published "Ghost Patrol" in *Forces Journal* in 2013; Jeffery Hess published "Soldier's Cross" in his *Home of the Brave: Somewhere in the Sand* anthology in 2013; and Erica Vital-Lazare published "Operation Battle Mountain" in *Red Rock Review* in 2014. Beyond merely publishing the stories, these editors each offered feedback and advice that made each story better.

Of course, none of this is at all possible without Justin Race and his team at the University of Nevada Press. They have been thorough, professional, and generous in helping me improve these stories. I am forever grateful for all they have done to bring this book to life, and I am so proud to be published through their press.

My family and friends helped me survive in a country during wartime, carried me through the years that followed, and helped me figure out how to put these words down. They include my parents, Gary and Charlotte Cage, my brothers, Zach and Charlie Cage, my sister Khalilah Cage, and my dear friend Rob McDonald. Of course, I owe everything and more to my wife, Brooke N. Cage, who has loved me and nurtured our two beautiful children, Charlotte N. and Arlo G. Cage, so that their lights can shine always, but especially when I need them the most.

Introduction

There are two kinds of books I will always read:
those about Nevada and those of the wars in Iraq
and Afghanistan, particularly Iraq. I started loving the literature of my home state when I was about
twenty, when I truly started to understand what
it meant to be a Nevadan. And by the time I was
thirty, after returning from my second tour in Iraq,
I started following the literature of the recent wars
more closely. Very often my favorite kind of literature combines both Nevada and these wars.

It happens more than I thought it would, the
cross-reference between the places, people, and
cultures that have meant so much to me in my life.
Sometimes the references are incidental. More
often, though, they seem to recognize something
subtle in describing the commonalities between
the two lands, and maybe more important, the

extraordinary differences.

Memoirs from these wars provide a lens for examining these similarities and differences. Reno native Matt Gallagher's memoir, *Kaboom: Embracing the Suck in a Savage Little War,* contains a few passing references to his hometown and his home state. My own memoir, *The Gods of Diyala: Transfer of Command in Iraq,* which I coauthored with Gregory Tomlin, has a chapter dedicated to a Halloween party in Reno. When I was home from Iraq for two weeks of leave in 2004, I gained an almost perfect awareness of how different my life and liberties were in my home country than in the Iraq I had just come from. Beyond these mentions, though, these memoirs are written by Nevadans, meaning that the state is woven into the narrative.

Jason Christopher Hartley provides an outsider's view in his memoir, *Just Another Soldier: A Year on the Ground in Iraq.* Hartley, an Utahn familiar with Nevada and its landscape, at one point ironically describes a palace in Iraq as not having as much class as a Vegas casino. Earlier, while he and his unit are driving through Kuwait into Iraq, he describes the scenery this way: "It was like driving through Nevada where there isn't *anything* for hundreds of miles, and then incredibly there will be families just chillin' off to the side of the road, usually with a herd of sheep or camels." As Hartley points out, both places are deserts, desolate at times but still inhabited by a rare type of people.

At some level, all of these memoirs explore the deep contrast between the pious cultures of the Middle East and libertine image and offerings of Nevada's biggest cities. Many would and do contest the accuracy of these generic assessments of the people and cultures of both Nevada and the Middle East, but these similarities and differences are at least broadly and subtly a part of the commentary of works like these. These generalizations mean something to the readers and writers who have experienced both. Or, as I think is clear by now, they mean something to me.

Literary fiction allows for more significant examination of these wars and the cities and high desert of Nevada. These works are not limited by the facts of the story like a memoir, and their authors

are not shy about using allusions to these similarities and differences as central images and themes
throughout their works. Instead of just describing
the differences, that is, these works of fiction allow
the authors to delve deeper and make real assertions
about mankind at its best and worst, located in
the discussion of the foreign and the familiar and
notions of home and the self.

As with the memoirs, a number of fictional works
about the wars in Iraq and Afghanistan merely mention Nevada in passing and do not spend much time
developing themes or characters around the state.
Siobhan Fallon's short story collection, *You Know When
the Men Are Gone,* contains a story called "The Last
Stand" that has a character who spent his summers
growing up in Winnemucca, Nevada, the mining
and agricultural town on Nevada's rural Interstate
80 corridor. Luke Mogelson namechecks Nevada in
his story "Peacetime" (from his collection *These Heroic,
Happy Dead*). Katey Schultz's *Flashes of War,* fiction and
flash fiction about the wars in Iraq and Afghanistan
from different perspectives, includes a story called
"Pressin' the Flesh," which features a route named

"Nevada Street" by American forces in Iraq.

While these are merely passing references to the state in wartime books, Jesse Goolsby's novel *I Would Walk with My Friends If I Could Find Them* makes exploring the differences between Nevada and the Middle East a minor theme throughout his book. He uses Nevada to show cultural differences at the beginning of the novel, as an Afghan interpreter explains to his US Army colleagues that when he leaves Afghanistan, he'll go to Las Vegas and become a dealer in a casino. The interpreter seems naïve about how difficult it will be to accomplish such a goal, but to someone already helping the enemy of the people of his home country, Sin City might represent the ultimate opportunity to depart from his home culture as well.

For Goolsby's American characters, Nevada represents another type of departure. As he describes it, Nevada is the type of place "to escape to after you've lived a life." His main character, who is from the northern California town of Susanville, breezes through Reno and Lake Tahoe on the Nevada side of the Sierra at different points throughout the book. Later, some of his other characters discover the tiny towns of Wells and West Wendover. One chapter is entirely set in the quiet, rural, northeastern mining town of Elko. These escapes into the different landscapes of Nevada happen throughout their young adult lives, but it is when they seek the quiet rural reaches of the state after their wartime service that we recognize the heart of Goolsby's statement that Nevada provides an escape "after you've lived a life."

Las Vegas-based writer Laura McBride doesn't spend much time on the obvious similarities of the landscape or the manifest differences in the cultures in her novel *We Are Called to Rise.* Instead, her work draws out the more subtle similarities of a shared trauma, whether it is from living in a country ravaged by war, or from abuse or neglect at the hands of a parent. She focuses on the American wartime experience, especially as it plays out in the families, neighborhoods, and settings of Las Vegas.

Because *We Are Called to Rise* is set in Las Vegas, a city built on hope and second chances, like that held by the Afghan interpreter in Goolsby's novel,

McBride makes her main point through a gambling metaphor, namely that no matter how bad things get, her characters, like so many, will still stand at the table of life and play. But really, *We Are Called to Rise* isn't about betting at all. It's about the choices people make in life no matter what trauma they have faced, and it is about having hope that one can keep doing better, keep living better, and keep getting better. The people of both Nevada and the places of our ongoing wars in Iraq and Afghanistan share this same need for hope; otherwise, life might not seem worth living at all.

It may seem simplistic or even absurd to compare the experiences and conditions faced by those who reside in a glitzy place like Las Vegas with the experiences of those who face death, hunger, destruction, and loss in Iraq and Afghanistan every day. But a child growing up in the stories of some of the best Nevada fiction around today probably has the same feelings of uncertainty as a child in a war-torn country, though the feelings may be based on vastly different perspectives. Just read the literature of the current crop of Nevada greats like Willy

Vlautin, Ellen Hopkins, H. Lee Barnes, or Claire Vaye Watkins, and you'll see plenty of struggling people, plenty of people needing hope. These are the people in McBride's pages, just as their counterparts are all over the pages of every book set during the wars in Iraq and Afghanistan.

The stories in *Desert Mementos* explore these same connections between Nevada and Iraq: the similarities in the landscapes of each desert, the contrasting cultures and worldviews, and the need for hope. Taken together, the stories represent the arc of a single, yearlong deployment, common for army soldiers during the recent wars. Themes and characters connect some of the stories, but what truly connects each story is the slightly varying perspective presented on my home state and my second home within the Middle East, and how these places change the concept of identity.

The collection begins with "Tonopah Low," which is set entirely in cities and towns in Nevada. The early stories that follow largely mention Nevada only in passing, much as happens in the works of Mogelson and Fallon. The middle stories, starting with "Operation Battle Mountain," bring Nevada to Iraq, and, at least in "Soldier's Cross," bring Iraq back to Nevada as well, if only for a short time.

As Goolsby writes, Nevada is the sort of place that a person should live after they have lived a life. As McBride might say, Nevada is also a place where a person can keep moving forward, no matter the trauma they have experienced and endured. *Desert Mementos* embraces both of these authors' points, ending the collection back in Nevada, their characters changed but hopeful.

DESERT MEMENTOS

1

Tonopah Low

THREE NIGHTS BEFORE your second deployment to
Iraq you finish a Michelob and slide the bottle back
in the box behind the passenger seat. You've only
been driving for less than an hour, so you decide
to switch to Copenhagen for a little while. There is
only one reason you can think of for a twenty-one-
year-old man to be driving from Reno to Tonopah
on a Friday night in weather like this.

Your phone rings, but you let it go. You've kept a
low profile while on leave, so it's probably your dad.
You can talk to him in the morning. You'll lose cell
coverage soon enough anyway.

You slow down on Highway 50 between Carson
and Silver Springs, but it's not just the piling snow
and the quiet streets that make you do it. A ticket
in rural Nevada on a night like you're having would
mean more than a fine and a few points. The Cut

Off will save you ten minutes if you can find it in the night and the snow.

You do and turn onto the two lanes of untouched powder. If it were daylight, you'd see ranches and open fields. You turn on your brights, and they illuminate the large flakes falling toward the ground more than the path forward. You turn the heat up. You turn the radio up. You lean forward in your seat, as if that will help you see better.

You met her back in high school. You were the mediocre athlete and she was the girl who was pretty but unnoticed. She was skinny and hid her muscular body under baggy clothes year-round. You were skinny, too, but even third stringers got toned muscles during football season. You try to recall how you met five years ago, but all you can remember was something about art class during your sophomore year. You both stayed beneath the radars of your worlds but not because you wanted to.

You and she used to argue about who had the worse family. You said yours, because your parents told you how great you were even though the evidence suggested otherwise. She said hers, because her mother kept bringing idiots around their apartment, sometimes dangerous idiots. You never told her about the time your dad said you could do better than her. Or later how he said that you were settling on the army just like you were settling on her. Somehow you couldn't bring yourself to do it. She told you later that she knew anyway, from how your dad treated her.

You spent your entire junior and senior years together. She came to your games and you dropped by the restaurant where she worked. You explored Reno together with your fake IDs. You climbed to Peavine Peak together and smoked a little. She snuck into your room when your parents were asleep. Her mom didn't care when you came or when you left.

She found a poem she liked by Rodney Jones in college and she called you that night to read it to you. She reread a line that she thought you would think was funny given all of your nights together in Reno:

And millennia would come and go, but not before
I fumbled my body to one girl in the back seat of a car

And drove through the countryside at a hundred twenty,
Praying to the stars to kill me or let her have her period.

It was funny, you said, and you both laughed about the scare you had waiting for the test to come back.

While you were at basic training she sent you a copy of *Things That Happen Once* with the page of that poem dog-eared. You read it every chance you got. The book was lost along with a box full of other household goods when you moved to Germany to join your artillery unit. You didn't think about it again until well into your first deployment to Iraq.

How to adjust the heater in your dad's truck is not intuitive, so you just turn it off when you get too warm. You'll have to turn it back on full blast later, unless you pull over and figure it out. You drop a lip full of cashed snuff out your window and hold your hand outside until your fingers are numb. You're moving slowly enough to see the dark wad fall straight through the piled snow.

You'll take Highway 95 the rest of the way to Tonopah and catch as many of the shortcuts as you can. You started hours later than you had hoped to and are still hours away. You keep passing mile markers, though slower than you'd like. You look at the dash clock and decide it has been long enough for another beer.

The guy on the radio says the snow will continue all night. Cold air coming down from Canada is hitting warm air coming north through the Great Basin in what he calls a Tonopah Low, causing the rare weather event you are driving through. Hawthorne might even experience blizzard conditions, he says, a merciful reprieve after years of drought in the eastern Sierra.

The highway is straight in front of you, and its steep grade nudges you to speed up. You push the gas a little harder, but not too much. You adjust your seat and then your mirrors. Your headlights are the only ones on the road.

You were seventeen when you joined the army, and with the moves, the distance, and the immediacy of the war, you called her less and less. You were nineteen when you returned from your first year-long tour in Iraq. She turned twenty before you did, and two weeks after her birthday she was married.

You shouldn't have lost touch. But by the time you moved to Germany the only time you thought of her was to remember the way her stomach muscles suggested a perfect waistline. There were plenty of others to distract you along the way anyway.

When you got back from your first deployment, the parties were mostly to celebrate not being in Iraq anymore. Those blurred with all of the parties for all of the guys you served with who were headed back to the states one at a time. Both ended the same, with a bunch of drunk crewcuts sitting around talking quietly about Jimenez, about Cantrell, about that kid in the market, and about everything else.

You heard she was pregnant from the same high school friend who told you she was married. The drinking made you jealous, but that didn't mean you were happy when you heard she lost the baby at seventeen weeks. It made you angry, actually, but so did everything.

The snow is still beating up 95, covering the road and everything under your headlights. You slide into a curve in the road but you recover easily. You miss the turn for the wildlife refuge that would have bypassed Yerington and let you save another fifteen minutes. You decide to stop drinking for the rest of the trip and settle for more Copenhagen for something to do.

Even though you would have preferred to skip it, at least Yerington is halfway. It looks nice at night. All of Nevada looks nice at night, and especially when it is covered in fresh snow. It looks like renewal, even if you know it will be gone in a day or two.

Hawthorne is straight ahead, but still several hours away at this pace. You check your cell phone even though you know you lost coverage long ago. The snuff tastes fresh and you let the dark spit build in your mouth until you have to swallow it, just to keep you awake at least until Hawthorne. Maybe it will help cover your breath if you get pulled over, too.

You were back in Germany for three months when you finally reached out to her again. You didn't leave a message the first few times you called, but you finally reached her. Even if she mentioned her husband three times, she seemed relieved to hear from you.

Eventually she told you her husband was a loser. He wanted her to get pregnant, even while she was going to college and waitressing to support the family. He couldn't work, because he was writing a novel and had been for a few years. She told you that he said the miscarriage gave him a new idea for his plot. She said she was always her own mother growing up, and now she was his too.

You told her you were fine when she asked, just scrapes and bruises. When she pressed, you distracted her with all of the crazy stories about you and your idiot friends in Germany—about the night you pissed in front of the police station, the night you wore your combat helmet to dinner at one of the nicer restaurants in town, or about the times you and your friends would engage random Germans in political discussions just to watch them recoil. "Don't you think George Bush is awesome?" your friend Trevor would ask to their horror.

You told her about the German girls. You told her about your friends who were going home. You were blacking out several days a week and dreaming of ways to make it stop, but you didn't tell her about that.

She figured it out on her own, at least the broad strokes. Of course she did. It was always a part of the background to your stories, she told you. She knew when you were drunk on the phone, too, but she said it made sense. You'd just survived a year in Iraq. You told her the army thought it was only natural, too, unless you were driving or beating your spouse. She finished the joke for you, saying it was a good thing you didn't have a car or a wife.

You drive along the foothills toward Hawthorne. There is still no blizzard, but the wind is blowing the snow across Walker Lake. The empty police cruiser that's been sitting beside the entrance to the Paiute Reservation for years still spooks you, but you aren't even going forty-five miles an hour.

As you pull into Hawthorne you slow to the posted speed. It's quieter than Yerington, but more of the businesses are open. Stopping now will only slow you down. And besides, you have plenty of gas and the Copenhagen is keeping you awake for now. You remember the truck route that handrails the

Hawthorne Army Depot storage site and you take it, skipping the few traffic lights in town.

Years ago you stopped on this stretch of road with her when you drove her to Vegas for college. You stopped at a sign dedicating portions of the highway to those who fought in World War II, and you took a picture of her in front of it for her grandfather. You stopped and took another in front of the sign for Korean War veterans when she realized she couldn't remember which war her grandfather had fought in. As you drive the road tonight, you see that they have added a sign for those who fight in your war and the one in Afghanistan.

It's a hundred miles from your sign to the Tonopah Station, give or take. If you had to guess, you'd say that the roads were getting marginally better, but not enough to get you there any faster. There are no more cutoffs either, so you go back to counting mile markers.

You grab another beer, but decide better of it and put it back. Snuff will sustain you. You'll need a clear head on the other side of this drive. You'll need the sum of your strength.

You haven't seen a car since Yerington. You look up to catch some of the night sky of central Nevada, but there is only swirling snow. You push it back up to forty-five, then to fifty. That will have to do for at least a while.

When you told her you were coming home on leave before your next deployment she said she wanted to come see you in Reno. You turned her down at first, but none of your reasons made sense, not even to you. At the end of the week, she said she still wanted to see you. She suggested you meet in Tonopah, halfway between Reno and Vegas. You could stay at the Station where the two of you spent your last trip together; maybe stay two nights if she could come up with a good enough lie to tell her husband. You and she could relive your high school days, but this time, she said, you would have to be more careful.

You wanted to see her. You were willing to drive hours in a snowstorm to make it happen. But as much as you wanted it, you didn't want her to see you. You knew you were different from the person she used to love, and not in many good ways.

You actually told her that when your excuses ran out, but she didn't buy it. She told you to stop beating yourself up, that you had always been shamed by impossible standards and imperfections. She said to bring the old you to Tonopah, even if that smiling young face was harder to come by anymore.

By the time you agreed on Friday afternoon you had already had too many drinks. You napped and sobered up as much as you could. You bought a twelve pack and left her a message that you were on your way. It is six hours later when you pull into the Tonopah Station.

You check your eyes in the rearview before getting out of the truck. You look clammy and tired and you feel the same. You put the rest of the beer in your duffel bag and head in.

The clerk tells you she hasn't checked in yet. You grab some hash and eggs at the diner, making sure you are facing the entrance and making sure your coffee cup is empty when the waiter walks by. The doors let in the cold air each time they swing open, and even though only a few guests arrive after you, it is enough to drive you to your room.

You plug your phone in but there's still no signal. You dial her number from the room phone and she answers, only to tell you quietly that she'll call you right back. When she does and the front desk connects you, she tells you she's not coming. She tried calling you, she says, but it kept going straight to voicemail.

You are angry, but you keep it together. You tell her that you drove a long way to see her. You tell her that the snow was hammering the north part of the state, but she should be fine coming from the south. You tell her that you found your copy of *Things That Happen Once* and that you brought it with you so you can read it together again. You read her the line from "A Prayer to the Goddess," and when she is silent, you read her the whole poem.

She tells you that you and she aren't those kids anymore. She tells you that you can't have things just because you want them. She tells you it's never been that way.

You tell her that you are that kid again, the old you, the one you both wanted to see again, for the first time in two years. You tell her that it is all because of her and that you want to stay that way. She calls you Bucky for the first time since before you left for Germany and she tells you she doesn't want to be one last escape for you before you go back to Iraq on Monday.

2

Ghost Patrol

HE LOOKED BACK through the doorway as he exited, checking to make sure that he had all he needed. He patted the chest of his body armor for his glasses and felt all seven magazines in his ammo pouch. He took a deep breath and walked to the line of vehicles where his guys were waiting.

He was nervous because he was going to be addressing the Ghost Platoon as their leader for the first time since they became responsible for AO Vegas. He could feel it in his chest. It made his saliva heavy, ruining the Copenhagen he had packed into his lip, making him wish he had filled the CamelBak that his commander had made everyone zip tie to their green flak vests.

He had never worn more gear than this. He cursed at how the gravel shifted under his feet with the weight. He could hear generators running and he could smell their fuel, but he still had no idea where they were on the base. Before he rounded the last corner between him and his guys he stopped in his tracks, realizing that he had left his can of dip sitting on the small wooden box he was using as his nightstand. He hit the illumination button on his watch—0300. He had plenty of time to head back to his room before their patrol. He cursed his lack of rituals as he walked back to his room.

By the time he got back to his line, his guys were waiting for him. Roughly arranged by squad, they were dressed in mismatched desert and woodland camo, their new combat gear hanging awkwardly off their flak vests. A few of them were leaning quietly against their trucks, and a couple of the younger guys were horsing around and laughing loudly. He recognized their anxiety, and wondered briefly how it was manifesting in himself. His platoon sergeant, Clemens, a young man from Kentucky, walked up and handed him the paperwork: 0415, three-hour patrol in AO Vegas, four vehicles, twenty troops. He signed it and Clemens sent a runner from the platoon to the battalion TOC to turn it in.

He headed toward his truck, an M1114 up-armored Humvee that carried five—two soldiers in the back passenger seats, a gunner protruding from the top, his driver and him in the front seats. The trunk space was packed with body bags and stretchers, and the signs and concertina wire they regularly used to shut down traffic. The metal well between the two back seats was filled with crates and cases of ammo. Each of the four trucks in Ghost Platoon was wrapped in armor and had armored glass.

"Talon X-ray, Talon X-ray, this is Ghost 6, radio check, over," he said into the battalion hand mic.

"Ghost 6, Talon X-ray, lima charlie, over," a bored voice came back over the radio, using a shorthand for loud and clear that was forbidden and wouldn't have been used if there was anyone above a captain awake at this hour.

"Roger that, Talon X-ray, Ghost 6 out," he said, allowing himself to break from protocol a bit as well. He switched to his platoon frequency and called for another radio check. Sergeants Johnson and Thomas, his first and second squad leaders, answered clearly, and Sergeant Clemens's driver answered that the platoon sergeant was handling some issue to do with a tow bar.

A green flare shot into the sky from the west, followed closely by a red flare. At first he thought they were tracers, but they slowed as they reached their apex and drifted before they burned out. He had seen them every night since he had arrived three weeks before, just as he had heard loud explosions in the city when he knew no American forces were out on the road. The flares seemed more personal now, but that didn't mean he could make any more sense of them.

"Comms are good, V," he said to his driver, who was responsible for making sure that he could talk to battalion and to the rest of his platoon. "Crystal clear."

"We got lucky, sir," Specialist Valdez said, trying to figure out how to align his night vision goggles with his right eye. "The Fourth ID guys gave us all of their excess radio equipment before they left and a lot of it was brand new."

"All through training at Hohenfels and Graf our comms sucked," he said. "I actually thought they were supposed to sound like they had something living in them."

"These ones work pretty good," Valdez said.

He left the driver alone after that. Valdez had more responsibilities than most in the platoon, and he had obviously been working for several hours to make sure everything was going to go right once they headed out of the wire. Maybe he was worried that he wasn't going to have time to get his NVGs adjusted in time, he thought. Maybe he was just worried.

"Thanks for getting everything ready to go, V," he said, and walked away, not waiting for a response.

Sergeant Clemens walked up to him, contemplating fresh grease on his hand. They had a brief discussion confirming that everything they could think of was complete. They exchanged head nods to confirm that they were ready. He walked back to his Humvee in the front, which was running, lights on. Harrison, his gunner, was posted in the hatch, while Valdez smoked a cigarette outside the door.

"Ghost Platoon, Ghost Platoon, radio check, over," he said into his platoon mic, and received clear responses from his squad leaders and from Clemens. At his next transmission they began moving the several hundred meters toward the operating base's only entrance and exit. "This is Ghost 6, break," he said next. "Let me know when we're red, over." He charged a round into his M4, then listened to make sure everyone in the other three vehicles were doing the same.

He paused, wondering if it was nerves or the heavy body armor that was causing the tightness in his chest. He tapped the can of tobacco in his right cargo pocket and keyed the radio mic.

"Talon X-ray, this is Ghost 6, over," he said into the battalion frequency.

"Ghost 6, go ahead, over," the answer came back, even lazier than it had been before.

"Talon X-ray, Ghost 6, break," he said, releasing the button on his mic. "Ghost Platoon SP FOB Warrior time now, over."

"Roger, out," came the bored reply.

Valdez pressed down on the gas and moved them slowly onto the blacktop of Highway 1, headed west. He always thought he would sound different, more confident, more in command the first time he announced his platoon's entrance into the combat zone. He had hoped his voice would be more gravelly, his tone more grizzled. But he sounded like himself, hiccupping slightly from the tobacco juices he had had to swallow and trembling from everything in his head.

A few seconds later Clemens radioed to say that all four of the vehicles were on the road. As they started to hit their stride down Highway 1, two more flares, this time red then green, burst above AO Vegas. He slapped the gunner's leg, asking him if he was hearing anything out there. Negative, just some homemade power lines crackling overhead and a few dogs howling. He asked the same of his sergeants over the radio, but they couldn't hear anything from behind their bulletproof glass either. He called in his second checkpoint to X-ray, and told Valdez the communications were still perfect.

AO Vegas was basically the southern half of the city, south of Highway 1, which ran through the city from east to west. AO Reno sat to the north. Someone at battalion had decided to name the areas of operations after the two major cities of his home state. The battalion operations officer said it would give the guys a taste of home when they were out on patrol, a statement that made some of the lieutenants roll their eyes. In actuality, there were six or seven smaller villages, each with proper names, histories, and identities.

The convoy turned south off of the highway, which was really only a four-lane road that bisected the city, and he told X-ray where his platoon was. They were conducting their presence patrol, serpentining through the small villages in their AO at five miles an hour or so, looking for curfew breakers, insurgents, or anything else that looked out of place. The only time he had been through this village before was during the daytime, when it didn't look at all daunting or dangerous. At night, through the green filters of night vision goggles, every shadow looked darker, every parked car looked weighted down like a car bomb.

Once they turned off of the main road, they had no set course. He would push his platoon in any direction he chose, trying his best to never retrace a path. It would be easy to decide where to go if there was gunfire or explosions in any part of the village, but with nothing but a few errant flares, he had nothing to move toward, nothing to chase.

He told Valdez to take a sharp turn down a narrow dirt road between two small mud brick houses. They couldn't see very far down it, but it looked passable, and it looked like there was some ambient light twenty meters down or so. They moved slowly at first, tentatively. Valdez showed his unease for the first time, but kept the Humvee moving forward in the absence of any new instructions. They rocked in their seats when their right tires slid into a shallow trench but were able to keep moving forward even at the new angle.

He looked out his window at the lifeless homes mere inches from him—not a light or a curious set of eyes visible through the cloth curtains. He settled back in his seat, hoping they would be able to make it through the narrow alley to the other side when the gunner Harrison dropped through the hatch into the back, covering his head. "Antenna's catching and sparking, sir," he said.

The houses were connected by a web of power cords, some looking like they had recently been attached to a toaster or coffee maker, held up by long branches, at best, or by metal tent poles at worst. On the main road the makeshift power lines were higher, but in this alley they were low enough to catch the long, metal radio antenna on the back of the Humvee and mess up their communications.

"Can you grab it?" he asked Harrison.

"Yeah, hang on," said the gunner, already lifting himself up and out through the hatch and then walking down the back of the Humvee.

"Hope he doesn't shock himself," Valdez said, without a hint of the disdain that he usually had in his voice when he talked about the gunner.

"He's fine," the platoon leader said, watching Harrison wrestle with the antenna through his rearview. "Ghost Platoon, Ghost 6, break," he said into his platoon mic. "We've got low wires overhead in this alley, break. Get your gunners to jump out and pull your antennas forward until we get through this, over." Clemens responded that he had tied his down before they left the base, and apologized that he hadn't made the whole platoon do the same.

"No worries," the platoon leader said. "There'll always be another patrol." Valdez's seven-mile-per-hour pace made him confident that they could make it through the alley now that the antennas were down, a confidence that grew when the nose of his own Humvee poked out into a cross street twice as wide and with electric cords twice as high. He exhaled when Clemens confirmed that all of their vehicles were back on the road and matching Valdez's self-assured ten miles per hour. His voice was crisp when he called in his platoon's coordinates to battalion. His mind was clear when he ordered Valdez to speed up toward the two green flares that shot into the air a few hundred meters to their direct front.

He was sitting forward in his seat when they got to their best guess of where the flares had originated. Valdez slowed down without having to be told. The platoon leader pulled the Copenhagen from his cargo pocket, packed it with his forefinger, and pushed a tight lump of it into his mouth. He asked Harrison, but the gunner wasn't hearing anything. He called into X-ray, but they confirmed that no one was reporting anything unusual within sector.

He knew that whoever had shot the flares, or had been shooting the flares all night, was probably staring down at him from a rooftop on this or some other nearby street, and was not going to present himself when a four-vehicle convoy crawled down his street. He stared down into a garbage bucket that had been pulled down off of the sidewalk and onto the street. He told Valdez to speed up a little bit as they pulled back onto the blacktop that would take them deeper into the villages of AO Vegas. He swallowed a thin steam of tobacco juice and called in their latest coordinates to a barely awake Talon X-ray. Valdez broke a smile when the platoon leader pinched Harrison hard on his inner thigh when the gunner started to announce the presence of fictitious insurgents to their front, pretending their boring first patrol was more exciting than it really was.

They rounded the city blocks and moved toward daytime market areas throughout AO Vegas. They were unopposed, free to move without any concern. He had faith in their thick windows, their armor, and their vastly superior weapon systems. He knew that he and his guys had been trained as well as they could have been and that the will to survive would take care of the rest.

"Talon X-ray this is Ghost 6, RP FOB Warrior time now, break," he said as his platoon pulled through the gates outside their base. "Negative contact, nothing significant to report, over."

"Ghost 6, roger out."

He wished they had arrested the guy who was taunting them with flares. He wished they had killed someone planting a bomb on the side of the road. He watched as his guys cleared their weapons at the barrels inside the wire. And he wished he knew which ones were going to die. But he also knew they would spend their whole year fighting a phantom they would rarely get a chance to confront, and that even if he took his whole platoon home, it would be only a mere shadow of what it was tonight.

3

Desert Island

GUARD TOWER DELTA had an American flag painted
on its front in desert colors. It rose from the Iraqi
soil like an American-made minaret. A key piece of
the base's defense system, it was a monument vul-
nerable to attack. At sixty feet, constructed of iron,
the tower protected a quarter of the base's perimeter. The soldiers called it "Desert Island" less
because the phrase corresponded with the same let-
ter and more because it faced a vast expanse of desert to the east.

Corporal Cory Johnson and Specialist John
Pierce were on late-afternoon guard shift. This was
the worst shift they could have drawn because of the
afternoon heat. To be on a shift together made it
even worse because they hadn't spoken in months.

With only four towers, and twenty-nine junior
soldiers in their platoon, they rarely had to pull

guard duty together, a fact that suited both of them just fine. When they did, Johnson did his best to ignore Pierce. Sometimes he even broke regulations and brought his headphones up to the tower and listened to country music during their shift. They had been there for six punishing hours. There were two more to go.

"What's that guy doing out there?" Johnson asked, breaking his silence for the first time.

Pierce, surprised that Johnson was talking to him, said, "I was wondering the same thing."

About two hundred meters in front of them an Iraqi man in a white robe and headscarf had stopped and raised the hood of his car. He had been driving across the open desert in a red Renault when smoke began pouring from the hood. When he got out of his car, he waved to them and pointed to the smoke coming out from under his hood. He held both of his hands in the air, and then focused his energy on his car.

"You think he's a threat?" Johnson asked in a low voice. "Should I fire a warning shot?"

"If I lived here, I'd never leave that question in

anyone's mind," Pierce answered.

"Are you being tough or cute, Pierce?"

"I was just saying," Pierce said defensively.

"I was just saying, *corporal*," Johnson said. The last time they had pulled guard together they were both specialists, but Johnson had been promoted to corporal since, making him a junior noncommissioned officer.

"I was just saying, corporal," Pierce said.

"Well, what do you think?" Johnson asked, trying to lighten his tone.

"What about, corporal?" Pierce answered.

"Do you think I should fire a warning shot?"

"You are just going to have to explain why you are one round short when they do the shakedown after this shift, corporal. There's going to be an investigation is all I'm saying."

"You saying that you wouldn't back me up, Pierce? You wouldn't say that that guy is a presumed threat and I had to take a shot to move him along?" Johnson asked, still focused on the man near the car. "I guess I shouldn't be surprised."

"That's not what I'm saying," Pierce said.

"I mean, I could probably just shoot a window out right now and he'd get the picture. I could always just say you did it," Johnson said, bringing his carbine up and aiming down his iron sights at the man below them.

"Are you going to do it?" Pierce asked.

Johnson kept the M4 up, squinting through its sights. He rested his elbow on the railing of the tower and pulled the buttstock tight to his shoulder. Then he relaxed his grip and lowered the rifle so he could closely examine its settings. He switched the rear sight to day aperture and extended the buttstock about an inch before repositioning his elbow on the railing and bringing the rifle back up to his eye again. That high up, and that far out in the open, there should have at least been a slight breeze, but he noticed nothing.

"Remember last year, Pierce?" he asked quietly, steadily, with his mouth breathing on the hand that held the pistol grip. "Remember that night you went out drinking with your friends in Vegas and you banged that girl from Barstow?"

The Iraqi man in the desert in front of them

stopped working on his engine and was looking up at them now. He shielded his eyes with his left hand and then waved both of his hands over his head. "You remember that night, right? Her husband was stuck working a rotation at Fort Irwin. No one would ever know. All you had to do was get her alone, right? You remember that night, don't you?" He was still looking down the sights, speaking in a voice so low and calm that he was surprised when Pierce acknowledged him.

"Of course I remember that night, Cory," Pierce said, turning fully toward the man next to him in the tower. "I'm sorry, I truly am. Put that down, let's just talk about this."

"What exactly could you have on your conscience that you want to talk about?" Johnson asked without raising his voice.

"I'm serious. I've wanted to apologize about that night since it happened. Put the gun down. You're just terrorizing that guy out there," he said, pointing out over the open space in front of Desert Island. As he pointed, the Iraqi man dropped his tools and ran around to the far side of his car.

"Look at that," Johnson said, a slow, slightly high-pitched laugh taking over his voice. "He thinks you are giving me the order to shoot, doesn't he? Do it again. Point out there again and see what happens."

"Knock it off, man," Pierce said again.

"He is just sort of trapped, isn't he?" Johnson asked quietly, still holding his smile from before. "He's trapped by all that open space. He can't go anywhere. He just has to sit there and take it," he said, following the man with his sights as he moved back and forth behind the car, waving his hands whenever he popped his head up.

"He didn't do anything, Cory. Just let him fix his car and go home to his family."

"He didn't do anything? He has a family?" Johnson asked. "How do you know that, John? How do you know he didn't screw his friend's wife one night? We don't know this guy. He could be a real lowlife. Maybe he deserves some retribution."

"Cory, I'm sorry. We were out in Vegas when we ran into her and her friends. We were drunk and so were they. We danced together."

"And then what, John? You forgot she was my wife?" Johnson asked, surprising himself that he was able to keep his voice as quiet and steady as it was when he started the conversation. He adjusted his sweaty hand on the pistol grip on the lower receiver of his rifle, moving his finger from the trigger guard to the trigger for the first time. "Was it just because you could, John? Did you know we were having trouble?"

"I don't know what I was thinking, Cory. It just happened."

"You think?" Johnson laughed, his weapon rocked with his emphasis, but he quickly retrained on the man out front of them.

"Listen, Cory, I'm so sorry. I'm ashamed of myself. We are all supposed to be brothers here," John said.

"What do you guess he is doing now?" Johnson asked. The man had taken off his white headscarf and was holding it up in the space between his opened hood and his windshield. "You think he wants me to see if I can hit that, John?"

"Don't, Cory. Just put it down."

"I think he wants to see if I can hit it," Johnson said again. "Why else would he hold it up?"

Johnson took his finger back off of the trigger and dropped his hand to his grimy pants to wipe the sweat off. Sweat was running down the tip of his nose, too, but he was used to that. He was still leaning forward, resting on the railing, refusing to look at the other man. "Give me your scope, Pierce."

"What are you talking about?" Pierce asked.

"I don't trust this guy and I can't see him without a scope," Johnson answered.

"You can see him fine," Pierce said. "He's not a threat. Just leave him alone."

"Give me your scope."

"What are you going to do?" he asked.

"I haven't decided yet," Johnson said, taking Pierce's rifle and bringing the scope up to his eye, setting his elbow on the railing and pulling the buttstock of Pierce's rifle to him. "There he is," Johnson said. Johnson pulled on the charging handle slightly and opened the dust cover, rolled the weapon and checked the chamber, then released the handle and looked into the scope once again.

"I just want you to know this, Pierce," he said, exhaling to steady himself. "We are not brothers. We kill much, much better men than you all the time in this country. I know my wife was party to your game in Vegas, but I think you'll understand if I find her slightly easier to forgive." He clicked the selector lever from "safe" to "semi" with his thumb.

The man was moving behind the vehicle again. Then he came into full view, moving frantically, running in unpredictable directions. There was still no breeze. Johnson exhaled again, finding that perfect trough between breaths, that perfect sight picture that meant all he had to do was pull smoothly on the trigger.

4

Proxy War

THE EXPLOSION SHOOK the walls of my temporary office in the Baqubah government building. I felt it in my jaw, but knew the multiple brick walls and our wire perimeter kept the suicide bombers at a distance. I was worried about shrapnel hitting my guys pulling guard on the roof until the radio traffic reported no injuries. I got onto the battalion network and gave headquarters the update: another car bomb, this one between our building and the police station across the street. Nobody but the driver was hurt.

This had been the fourth car bomb of the year near the government building and it was only March. Two of my guys walked with me outside the gate to meet Lieutenant Dwyer and the Second Platoon, which had been dispatched by battalion to do the mop up. Sergeant Johnson was their squad leader. Stocky and loud, his helmet and flak vest darker than the rest of his uniform from grime and tobacco spit, you could always find him in a crowd. He was already near the gate, pointing a digital camera toward the ground, a mischievous smile on his face.

"Look, sir, it's a dick!"

"Sure enough," I said. Noticing a civilian woman in Kevlar gear standing behind him, I said, "Maybe you should be making sure your guys are pulling security instead of impressing this lady with your gallantry, Johnson."

Johnson ignored me and kept taking pictures. He showed one to the woman. She was wearing a salmon-colored shirt and blue pants under a woodland camo vest and blue helmet. She looked ridiculous in her mismatched gear, which hung crooked and loose. She laughed as Johnson zoomed in, then she slapped his shoulder when he said something else.

"She the reporter?" I asked Dwyer, walking to the other side of his Humvee.

"That is indeed sweet Anne Reynolds, but she

prefers to be called a 'journalist,'" Dwyer said.

Dwyer's platoon had picked her up in Balad and brought her to Baqubah a few weeks before. She had remained with the battalion since. Major Buehler, the battalion operations officer, had ordered everyone to give her access. "This is hearts and minds shit back home," he'd said.

"She's pretty hot," I said to Dwyer, staring at her while she laughed with Johnson.

"She gets a little uglier every time she opens her stupid mouth," Dwyer said, spitting a stream of tobacco onto the ground.

"I don't know," I said, admiring the way her bare neck looked with her dark hair tucked up into her crooked helmet. "I could get used to it."

"She's an absolute idiot and Buehler's letting her get too close to the guys," Dwyer said. "I'm actually pretty nervous about what she's going to write about us when she's done here."

"Hey sir, check this out," Johnson said, walking toward us holding what looked like a salad bowl.

"That better not be another dick," I said.

"No, it's a face, sir. I found it over there." He

tilted the bowl so we could see. It was the skin from the bomber's face—a neatly detached mask from jawline to hairline, with the red lining of once full lips, dark eye holes, a flattened nose devoid of cartilage, all sitting in a small pool of blood.

"Disgusting," Dwyer said.

"His dick's right over there, too," Johnson said. "No real loss, though. He would have just disappointed those seventy-two virgins anyway," he added, like a proud second grader.

"What are you going to do with it?" Dwyer asked. "I don't want to see you wearing it as a battle mask."

"Or strapped to the front of your Humvee for your next patrol," I added.

"I'm putting it in the body bag with the rest of his pieces," Johnson answered.

"Please tell me Reynolds didn't get pictures," Dwyer said.

"She didn't bring her camera today," Johnson said, walking away.

"It's a good thing he's tactically competent," I said when Johnson was out of earshot.

"He's good, but ever since she got here, he's lost

his damn mind," Dwyer said.

"He nailing her?" I asked.

"I don't think so. But Buehler is insisting she get all of the one-on-one time she wants." We stood there looking at her writing in a spiral notebook braced against her knee as the guys picked through car parts, body parts, and other debris. "When are you done with this rotation?" Dwyer asked, nodding to the government building.

"Fourth Platoon relieves us tonight," I said.

"Dinner?"

"Sure," I said.

We missed each other at dinner, but I saw Dwyer the next night. He was shaking his head as he walked toward me. "I'm sorry," he said setting down his tray. "For dinner?" I asked. "No worries."

"You didn't hear?" he asked. "Johnson had an accidental discharge last night."

"I thought we called them negligent discharges now," I said.

"Negligent, premature, accidental, I don't really care," Dwyer said. "Johnson had one when we got back in and Buehler assigned you the 15-6 investigation."

"It's not like I have a lot else going on," I said, shoveling green beans into my mouth. A formal 15-6 would determine what happened and make recommendations for discipline. It would take some time, but it wouldn't be too bad. I ate some potatoes and took a drink. "Johnson?" I asked when it finally settled in that such a good soldier had made such a mistake. "That doesn't sound like him."

"I've been ordered not to discuss it until after your investigation is complete," Dwyer said.

"Yeah, but really," I said.

"He left his magazine in," Dwyer said in a low voice. "Total amateur hour. I'm telling you, he's lost his mind."

"Dude's a damn squad leader," I said. "This is not going to end well for him."

We changed the subject. I told Dwyer about the government building and he told me more about Reynolds. There was no telling what she'd write. There was no telling the damage she'd cause.

After dinner, I went back to my room and sat

down at a desk made from stacked cardboard boxes with a piece of plywood I'd found for a top. My room was dark, and everything in it was some light shade of tan. It smelled, but I liked being back. I liked being away from the cramped government building. I liked not having to share one internet connection. I liked the quiet. Patrols would start back tomorrow.

I plugged in a flash drive and went through my pictures trying to find one to post on my blog. I'd started a blog a few months ago for the families back home. It was full of pictures of my guys out on routine missions, pulling security for the commander, or helping to build a police station. For today's post, I used a picture of them accompanying a Civil Affairs team handing out soccer balls to some of the kids around here. They even played a game. My guys, bulky with their Kevlar gear, were getting dominated by a handful of shoeless Iraqi preteens on a dirt lot littered with garbage. The photos were full of smiles, full of the hearts and minds imagery—all the things my command wanted us to share with those back home.

Buried in a series of folders on my laptop was a file I'd named "column." It was a piece I was writing for an online newspaper started by a group of American expatriates in Moscow. They were smartasses. They mocked American and Russian politics without mercy, but they sometimes got to the truth of things. They had a big reach. When we first got to Baqubah, I sent an e-mail to one of the editors and pitched a war column to them and they gave me five hundred words a week. I told the editor I would write about Iraq from a soldier's perspective, about our interactions with the locals, about the absurdities of our impossible mission, and about the harsh realities of urban combat. It would be the opposite of my rosy blog posts to family and friends. They told me they would protect my identity. I still messed with my timeline and location so no one could pin the column on me. I read this first submission one last time and sent it.

I thought about relaxing but I had to get going on the 15-6 investigation. I found Johnson's platoon sergeant and got some details. I told him that at a minimum, I would need to interview Johnson and get sworn statements from two others. He said he could have Johnson in the dayroom for the interview in an hour.

In the dayroom I watched the news, wondering how long we'd have power. It was quiet—everyone must have been out on missions in the middle of the day. I changed the channel just as Reynolds walked into the day room.

"Is it okay if I join you?" she asked.

"Of course," I said. I leaned forward as far as I could on the collapsed couch, and stuck out my hand. "I'm Scott," I said.

"Yes, nice to meet you," she said, smiling vaguely.

"I met you out with Sergeant Johnson at the car bomb site the other day," I said.

"That's right," she said. "We all look so different out of uniform." She paused, then laughed. "I mean, out of body armor."

"I know what you meant," I laughed. "Sorry about Johnson, by the way. He really is an incredible soldier, but he has some boundary issues."

"Not at all," she laughed. "He's had me dying since I got here." She needed help getting on the wireless, so I gave her the password.

"Where are you from?" she asked, still typing and looking at her screen.

"I'm from Nevada," I said.

"Las Vegas?" she asked.

"No, Carson City," I answered. "Up north."

"The state capital," she said, admitting that it was in fact the only thing she knew about the city.

"Where are you from?" I asked.

"New York," she said.

"Do you actually live in the city?" I asked.

"Yeah," she said. "I have a loft in Tribeca."

"I have no idea where that is," I said.

"It's downtown," she laughed.

"How is it there? Is it nice or that gritty, you know, city feel?"

"It's a pretty desirable part of town to live in, I mean, if you ask me," she said. "But I'd never be able to do it on my salary. My dad has a lease on a place there, and I just live in it. I figure it's easier to be there even though all of my friends are out in Brooklyn."

"What does your dad do that he can afford just to

have an extra apartment in Manhattan?" I asked.

"He is an attorney. He's done very well and since I am an only child, he likes to keep me close," she said, looking up more often now. "Actually, the truth is, he was never around when I was growing up, so I think he got the place for me to sort of make amends, but under the guise of keeping me close to him." She closed her laptop and set it aside. "What do your parents do that they can afford a place in tony Carson City?"

"Let's see," I said, pretending that the question was harder than it was. "My mom is a cocktail waitress, and my dad is a world-renowned loser."

"Wow," she said, laughing. "He must be a real piece of work."

"I guess I shouldn't be so hard on him, but he's just such a dependable flake." I told her about my mom, about my high school job, and about the girl who was sort of waiting for me back home. I was pretty guarded, remembering what Dwyer had said about her. But she was sharing some of her personal stories, too.

"Was your father in the military?" she asked.

"Oh, God no," I said, coughing. "He told me once that he and some friends were against the Vietnam War so they burned their draft cards."

"That was pretty common, right?"

"I guess so, but it was why he told me that sort of pissed me off," I said. "He invites me out to dinner to tell me that he was trying to come to terms with this war after I was commissioned. It was one of the few times he actually followed through on his word to meet me. So we meet and he starts by telling me what a mistake he thought this war was. He said that he had really tried to come to terms with it, but he just couldn't do it, not even for me."

"What'd you say?" she asked.

"I mean, I laughed. This is the guy who took off before I was born and who never followed through on a single promise to me. I just said that this was just one of those things that made us different, and he just looked at me with his stupid, confused eyes."

"Did you see him again before you left to come here?"

"That was the last time I saw him, which is exactly what I am sure he wanted. He had arranged the meeting so that he could stake out the moral high ground and could walk away with a clean conscience." She was about to say something, I thought, but Johnson walked in and interrupted her. "You mind if I do an interview over there?" I asked her, nodding to the table in the corner.

"Not at all," she said. "I have to get out of here anyway."

I felt awkward sitting down to interview Johnson. The ceiling fan spun over our heads. I adjusted my chair and it scraped loudly on the concrete floor. Johnson wasn't moving at all. He had taught me a lot when I was a new lieutenant. Now he had to tell me what had happened.

"We got done with the car-bomb mission at the government building, and my squad was lined up at one barrel, clearing their weapons one by one." Johnson was now slouching in his chair. "My guys cleared their weapons like we have done hundreds of times, and I checked them like we have done hundreds of times. I didn't wait for anyone to check me like I was supposed to because I was tired and my head was somewhere else. I just did it myself.

I pulled the charging handle to the rear. I looked at the chamber. I rode the bolt forward. I switched it to 'semi.' I pointed into the barrel. I pulled the trigger and my weapon discharged. I'd left a loaded magazine in the well, so when I charged it, a round chambered. I take full responsibility."

When he saw that I stopped moving my pen he asked me to make sure that I wrote down his last statement. "I have to own this," he said. Hours before Johnson's discharge, he'd been playing grab-ass with Reynolds, showing her pictures of a suicide bomber's dick. But the whole time he had still managed to outwork his squad. Now he just looked broken.

After the interview, I walked to headquarters to check my patrol schedule. My morning the next day was clear, so I would have time to finalize my investigation. Dwyer's platoon sergeant handed me another envelope on my way back to my room.

"It's from Shepherd," he said. "He was standing right next to Johnson when it happened."

"What does it say?" I asked.

"Come on, sir" he said. "You know I don't want

anything to do with this."

"I'm trying to make sure they take it easy on him," I said as quietly as I could.

"You do what you got to do, sir," he said, and walked away.

Shepherd's statement matched everything Johnson said. I just needed to file the 15-6 and it would all be over.

A WEEK LATER, I woke up an hour before my in-progress meeting with Buehler on the 15-6 and about three hours before our next patrol. I took my computer into the dayroom to catch up on a few things. I pulled up my pictures, trying to find something for my blog, deciding on one of two of my guys having a chili-cheeseburger-eating-contest in the mess hall at the brigade headquarters at two in the morning. The others were sitting around them laughing at a story another one was telling, a story that would have made most of their parents hang their heads in shame.

I checked my email and it was full of angry messages from back home. Reynolds had left the week before and her story detailing her time with Dwyer's platoon had posted. Johnson got it the worst of anyone, no question. He came across like a sex offender, crass and rude. She even wrote about him taking pictures of the suicide bomber's dick, judging him harshly for his lack of humanity in dealing with the bomber's remains. She was marginally nicer to some junior members of the platoon, and she basically left Dwyer alone. She didn't write about my guys at all.

I was pretty astonished. She lived with these guys for three weeks and had developed strong relationships with many of them. Then she humiliated them. Sure, Johnson was a jackass, but he was a good soldier. Now his parents, divorced and living on opposite coasts, were going to have to share in their son's embarrassment.

During my meeting with Buehler he asked a few questions about the platoon's weapon-clearing procedures, and how they had changed from before the incident. "Did you uncover anything else besides what you just went over with me that might have led to Johnson doing something as stupid as this?" he asked.

"I didn't, sir. The stated purpose of my investigation was to determine why the negligent discharge occurred, sir."

"Relax," Buehler said, smiling but still not looking up from the report. "There is some information that I think should be covered in your report. Not directly, but it should shape how you deliver the information to the boss," he said. "A few days before the incident, Johnson found himself alone with Reynolds somehow," he said. "So he nails her, and rumors make their way back home. So Johnson's wife e-mails him and tells him she's leaving and taking the kids. He was distraught when they got back that night, so he watches his squad clear their weapons, and then bungles clearing his own," Buehler said.

"Will it help him with that battalion commander?" I asked.

"Might soften the punishment some if it were figured in somehow," he said. "I mean, the guy's under a lot of stress as a squad leader in combat anyway, and then you throw this into the mix?"

"I guess I just don't know how to address it," I said.

"I don't know how you are going to do it either," Buehler said, and turned away from me toward a pile of paperwork on the side of his desk.

THREE DAYS LATER I was still trying to write the report. To say Johnson had broken another regulation by sleeping with Reynolds wasn't going to help him, but it seemed like Buehler wanted it in the report. Looking at the draft, I heard what sounded like another negligent discharge at the gate. I hoped *that* 15-6 would be someone else's problem.

I tried to focus on the right facts for my report. No one was hurt. The squad leader was the first person to accept all of the blame. The soldiers were better served by having a competent sergeant who was willing to admit a fault than any number of other noncommissioned and commissioned officers currently serving in Iraq. Still, I was pretty sure that no matter what I put in it, the battalion commander would drop the hammer on Johnson. He'd probably lose rank, pay, and probably even his position, which was really the worst part.

I knocked on Buehler's door and walked in after

his curt response. He looked confused when I told him I had the report. He was standing at his desk, putting paper into a folder.

"Johnson's dead, man," he said. "Shot himself in the showers about an hour ago."

I didn't know how to respond, so I just stared at him, still holding my report.

"How did you not know that?" he asked. "The whole base has been in a frenzy. We shut down the internet. We sent out word through the chain of command. Christ, your platoon is on clean-up duty."

"I never got the word, sir. I was working on this," I said, holding up the 15-6.

"You better go find your platoon, lieutenant," Buehler said.

They were in the latrine finishing cleaning up the remains of their dead friend. The shower stall was almost clean, and there was a garbage can full of bloody rags, and the room smelled of disinfectant. Johnson's naked body was laid out on two benches that had been pushed together. His clothes were folded neatly and sat on a counter, his M16 cleared and lying beside them. A single shell casing stood straight up on top of the sink.

Most of my guys were standing around, except for two privates who were still scrubbing the stall and the floor in front of it. They acknowledged me when I walked in, but they didn't say anything. Finally, one of them said that a Mortuary Affairs team was on its way to collect Johnson's body and property. Dwyer and his guys were organizing his gear back in the barracks. There wasn't anything else to do.

I was furious when I got back to my room. Furious at Buehler for forcing Reynolds on all of us, and then trying to use me to weasel out of any responsibility through my investigation. Furious at Reynolds for who she was and what her writing did to people I care about. I sat down at my desk and wrote my last column:

"The Choice Is Clear"

I'm looking at two pictures. One is of a human face. It's not what you think, though. It's the skin from jawline to hairline, complete with lips, nose, and eyeholes. It's sitting in a plastic bowl in a small pool of blood. The owner of this face, or what's left of it, was killed driving a car bomb.

The other is a picture of a young sergeant, a very dear friend of mine. In this photo he is laughing hard, and like always, making everyone around him laugh too. He took his own life today.

Here's what I can tell you about the suicide bomber in the first picture, even though I don't know him. He was almost certainly Sunni. He was probably between the ages of 17-28. He was not an outcast, but rather a zealot, bent on defeating the occupation force in his country. He probably got up early this morning to load his car and to pray. And then he drove downtown all alone and blew himself up at 10:21 a.m.

I know the sergeant in the second picture well. He worked hard. He kept his men safe. He taught everyone around him, even me. And he trained his men to be extremely proficient in all of the small unit tasks that we use to kill guys like that suicide bomber. Recently, he got a little too close and a little too careless with an American reporter and she burned him. I don't just mean that she wrote a bad story about him, which she did, but in getting that story, she ruined everything that was important to him. He stepped into a shower stall this evening and shot himself. He didn't leave a note, but I know he took full responsibility for everything he'd done because that's the kind of guy he is. She, on the other hand, published her story and then got on a plane, leaving a mess for everyone else to clean up.

I'm not equating the two men in these photos. Though he was unsuccessful, one believed that his God wanted him to blow himself up at a crowded market, or a police station, or out in the middle of the desert for that matter, just as long as he took as many innocent men, women, and children with him when he did so. The other was more successful, but he believed that he had dishonored those he loved so badly that no punishment would have sufficed. He left behind a wife and children who likely would have found it in their hearts to forgive him if only they'd had that chance.

Staring at these faces today, one of a person I couldn't care less about and one who I love as a brother, I have to acknowledge to myself that I couldn't do it. I couldn't kill myself for a cause, whether it was something I perceived to be larger than myself or some personal failing. Whether you could or not is irrelevant. Ask yourself this instead, in a war like this, one that could decide the future of the world, who would you rather have fight for the survival of culture and society as you know it? These guys, who were willing to die for what they thought was right, or those of us who write the stories of these wars, choosing which facts you should know, and sometimes hiding behind a pseudonym.

5

Operation Battle Mountain

SECOND SQUAD was loading up our vehicles when I walked out to do my checks. Some of the guys were handing up heavy weapons through the gunners' hatches, while others were putting cases of ammunition in the backs of each Humvee. Private Kennedy was trying to make everyone laugh with his fake radio checks, but nobody was paying attention to him. He either didn't see me, or he didn't care.

I made sure the Humvees had the right load for our mission. The squad was to have taken out the signage, concertina wire, and tow bars we normally carried on our patrols to set up checkpoints and bring all of the breaching equipment, zip ties, empty sandbags, body bags, and ammunition we could load. The trucks looked good and aside from Kennedy, the men were focused, and even Kennedy always managed to get his head right by the time we rolled. There were still several hours of daylight left and the team leaders said everyone had eaten. They were ready.

I moved away to study the green book I kept in my cargo pocket. I thumbed it open to the operations order for tonight's mission—"Operation Battle Mountain."

Naming the mission after my hometown made me angry. The other squad leaders would say it was just a joke, but they didn't know that my wife was in Battle Mountain, out of contact after sending an e-mail that suggested trouble with her pregnancy.

I knew where their jabs were coming from. A few weeks ago our platoon sergeant, Sergeant First Class Kenyon, pulled me aside and told me that his marriage was falling apart and asked me to help him manage the platoon so that he could focus on communicating with his wife. Being unofficial assistant platoon sergeant would mean more work, but he would let me move into the only other private room in our platoon area. Of course, with the whole platoon living in an open bay stacked on top of each other, space was at a premium. Kenyon had a small room on one side of the bay while the identical room on the other side sat vacant for so long the guys had stopped asking if they could have it. I took the job but declined the room. But Kenyon insisted, asking again in front of the other squad leaders. They said it was fine since it would allow them to spread out more.

It wasn't fine. I pulled out the operations order and started reading it again. I had found the order sitting in an envelope on my camping chair when I returned with my squad from a twenty-four hour security detail earlier this morning. I knew the name of the mission was a dig at me. Since the room change, the other squad leaders had been giving me even more shit lately about being from Battle Mountain. They insisted on calling me "Battle Born" and referring to my hometown as "Nowhere, Nevada." They'd found pictures of Battle Mountain and the mining towns around it online—the picture of "BM" written on the mountainside, the annual armpit festival, and the weathered faces of the people who chose to live there.

Under the operations order was a printout of my

wife's e-mail, sent two days ago. The last line said, "We'll see what the doctor says about the babies in the morning."

I had to find an interpreter. Saif was the only interpreter I actually liked and I walked across the gravel to where our interpreters bunked. I knocked on the door to the trailer. I was about to knock again when the lock on the inside of the prefab clicked and the door slid open.

The smell of saffron hit me hard before I walked in. Saif sat on the couch reading a magazine. Two other interpreters were watching a small black-and-white TV.

"You working tonight, Saif?" I asked. I offered my hand to the Iraqi man I had grown fond of over the last six of months.

"Don't want to," he said, peering up at me over the top of his magazine.

"Right, I don't want to work tonight either," I said. "But how about it anyway?" Saif had invariably been there when it counted. He'd never tried to hide in the truck when we needed him in a house, never played both sides of the table, never worn a mask, and had even fought side by side with us a few times. On a mission like tonight's, I wanted him; we needed him.

"I really don't want to tonight, Tom," Saif said, looking straight at me.

"It's a big mission," I said quietly. "We have good intel this time. I think we're going to get him," I said, with more urgency.

"I can't be seen out there right now, Tom," Saif said, leaning forward. "It's too dangerous."

He set the magazine down and pulled a half sheet of paper out of his breast pocket. He unfolded it slowly. "My wife found this on the door to my home this morning." He held it out so I could see the red Arabic script. "It names my daughters and son. It says if I do not stop assisting the occupiers they will all be killed. They left this where my family sleeps, Tom."

"What are you going to do?" I asked, squatting down next to him and taking the paper from his hand.

"I don't know yet."

"Is there anything you can do?" I asked.

"This is my family, Tom," Saif said. "I will do whatever it takes to protect them."

"Of course," I said. "Do what you gotta do, man."

"When it is dark, I will go to them," he said, leaning back on the couch. "Take one of the others," he pointed to his fellow interpreters watching the Egyptian sitcom.

"Sure," I said. I stood and told the bald one to be outside at 2200. He asked about the mission, but I told him I'd give him the details then.

I went back to my room and stripped off my gear. I sat down feeling heavy from exhaustion. She'd sent no new messages, so I reread the last line of her most recent e-mail, two days old now.

When I received my deployment orders to Iraq, Tammy moved from Fort Campbell back to Battle Mountain. She'd be closer to home and closer to family. She'd have the support she'd need to raise our babies during my deployment. Her messages from there were always brief and cheerful. "Things are fine here." "We miss you very much." "We'll see what the doctor says about the babies in the morning" was something else, though.

I knew a change would come at some point, but I didn't know how or when. I'd felt it in myself, too. For the first few months, things were moving quickly here. There was so much to learn, so many adjustments, and no time make sense of anything. After six months, the routine let me think. With time to think the risks became clearer. I felt more what I was missing back home. Now I knew that every decision I made could have an impact on whether I would be there to see the babies grow up.

The brief paragraphs that followed the order described a standard raid on the home of Waleed Mohammed, the command's highest value target. They told us that Waleed was expected to be home with his wife and three daughters, ages five, seven, and eleven. In the typically banal prose of all assessments, it read: "Target is likely to be heavily armed and in a defensive posture when at his primary residence."

We'd gone after him on every mission since we'd arrived but had never caught him. The battalion we replaced had been tracking him for three months to no end. We knew his house was a compound on a hill, but every raid we'd run before was on a cousin's house, an associate's house, or some supposed safe house. Waleed was never at any of them.

Waleed's success at eluding us created a mythology about him. We heard he always drove a car wired with explosives and wore a suicide vest in case he was ever cornered. We heard that he was always well protected by bodyguards. But we also heard he traveled without bodyguards because he trusted only himself.

I CHECKED MY E-MAIL one more time before leaving. There were messages from folks who were just waking up stateside, but still nothing from Tammy. I packed away my computer, put on my gear and slipped the harness of my M4 over my shoulder.

Riding out of base we stayed off our radios and drove without lights, everyone using their night vision goggles. The plan was basic, we'd go in through the front door, break into teams, and secure each room to determine if he was there. The other squads would be positioned at likely escape routes.

We came to a palm grove at the base of a hill. I lost sight of the other squads as they broke off to their security positions. The platoon leader and Sergeant First Class Kenyon were about a klick away. I got out of my vehicle without saying a word to the other squad leaders. My squad spread into a shallow wedge formation, and we started moving slowly up the hill as soon as I started walking.

If I hadn't seen the place in daylight so many times and studied it in satellite images, I wouldn't know it was there. The house was large. It was unlike the village ones below, which were hovels with thick iron gates packed together in the small alleyways where children played around the flow of human waste and makeshift power lines. This house had a generator, plumbing and the ability to oversee what was below.

There were no lights and the grounds were silent. We moved through the palm trees on soft dirt. Our night vision goggles illuminated everyone in green. Jimenez moved Alpha team a dozen yards up and to the left. They knelt behind trees while Jackson brought Bravo team up on my right.

I brought my squad on line in front of the house, a few meters from the door. I tapped Jimenez and his guys moved to a position behind a parked car and a water tank outside of the house. Jackson had Kennedy breach the door before I was ready but I shouldered in first, my guys following.

In the front room of the house I thought I saw a figure moving in the dark but paused before I pulled the trigger. It was nothing. I tasted the burn of the tobacco juice I was swallowing, though I didn't remember putting any in before the mission. We had made our presence known in the house, but we were still working quietly, methodically. I pointed out the room to the right, and part of Alpha team entered easily through the flimsy interior door. I waited for shots but it was silent. Jimenez and I moved past Alpha team to check the other bedroom. The window was open and the bed on the floor had been made but the room was empty.

Jackson and Kennedy moved past us to check the roof. Kennedy yelled that they had someone, but I thought he was joking since it should have been

Jackson reporting. He wasn't. They had two guys in front of them in zip ties and prodded the pair down a set of stairs that led from the roof. They were in their twenties, skinny and scared. The one Kennedy covered had a cut over his right eye that was bleeding onto his shirt. The platoon leader came up with the interpreter when I radioed that the objective was clear, and they started interrogating the pair. I didn't have anything to see or say, so I took my squad back to the bottom of the hill as quickly as I could.

It was still dark when we returned to the base, but I could tell dawn was coming soon. I felt the exhaustion setting in on my eyes and temples. My guys were tired, too. We completed our postmission tasks quickly, and I told them not to remove the weapons mounts because I knew we could get away with it until we all had a chance to rest. I knew I wouldn't be able to sleep for a while. I walked over to the phone center. No answer from Tammy, so I called her mom.

"I got an e-mail about the babies, Cheryl, what's going on?" I asked as soon as she answered, knowing she would forgive me for being abrupt.

"Tom," she said, pausing. "Tammy didn't want to bother you with it until we had some answers."

"Her last e-mail was three days ago," I said as calmly as I could. I was upset, but I knew it wasn't Cheryl's fault.

"We lost one of the twins," Cheryl said after a pause. "Tammy had to go to the emergency room and have a procedure. She's been in the hospital until today. Hopefully the doctor will tell us what's going on with the other baby and if they will have to deliver it prematurely or . . ."

"Or what, Cheryl?" I asked.

"Or if the second baby will survive," she said. "We've been on pins and needles back here, Tom, you've got to understand."

"Just let me talk to her," I pleaded softly.

"She's on bed rest, Tom. She can't talk."

"Just give her the phone so I can tell her I love her, please," I said slowly, enunciating each word.

Cheryl paused again before answering. "She's upset, Tom. She doesn't want to talk to you right now."

"Wait, this is my fault?" I asked, but Cheryl was silent. She was silent for so long I hung up. The lights were off in the open bay where the platoon slept, so I walked to my room instead.

I pushed the door open and a folded slip of paper fell to the floor. The barrel of my M4 hit the ground hard as I bent to pick up the note. I turned on my lamp and sat back in my chair.

"Tom," it read. "I have arranged a ride for my family to Mosul in the morning. My cousins insist that we stay with them. I won't be back. I must protect my family and I can't do that while working with you. Thank you for your friendship, and goodbye."

I didn't expect Saif's note, but I wasn't really surprised either. I turned on my computer and my mind went back to Tammy. Was there something more I could've done? Would she write again when all of this was over?

Someone tried to open my door. I unlatched it and turned on the light.

"Did you hear the news?" Kenyon poked his head in. "They hit Saif's house tonight."

"Dead?" I asked.

"Yeah. Saif met Waleed's guys at his front door and they got him," Kenyon said. "He was a good interpreter."

I thought about the time I saw Saif off-duty at the market, trying not to make eye contact with me while he bought food with his family. "He was a good man," I said.

Kenyon nodded and said good night.

Still no Waleed and now no Saif.

We had six more months to chase the warlord. It seemed he'd always be a step ahead.

I thought about the hard choice Saif made tonight as I stared back at my screen and opened a new e-mail to Tammy.

6

This Is Not Burning Man

WHEN I GOT to the head of the line at the security booth on the footbridge into Al Faw Palace I handed Leo my ID badge and asked, "What's at stake in the war effort today?"

"The whole damn war is at stake today, LT," Leo said, laughing at my nightly question.

"He really said that? I guess we're in for it tonight."

"He was in a mood," Leo said in his Louisiana accent. "A. Mood."

Every night Lieutenant Colonel Johns made a minor scene about how long Leo took to process the badges. And every night he made some pronouncement about the stakes of the war. And every night Leo and I had some version of our exchange, no matter how much it held up the line of people waiting to start the night shift at the headquarters housed in the palace. Johns liked to point out that he had been the officer in charge of the Joint Operations Center in Baghdad and Leo liked to point out that Johns was really talking about how important he was. Leo then took a special pleasure in slowing down the line whenever he saw Johns coming.

Clearing security, I tucked my book under my arm and went inside, saluting the lieutenant colonels who were leaving the day shift, and who were not, apparently, saluting junior officers. I'd been on the night shift for nine months and even as a late-deployment cynic, I still had to admit that Al Faw Palace was an extraordinary place to work. It had marble everywhere, decorated ceilings, chandeliers, and endless references to Saddam. The palace was on a man-made island in a man-made lake that Saddam had stocked with unique species of carp and bass and named after himself. Now, though, it was the centerpiece of Camp Victory, which included several operational bases and Baghdad International Airport. It was also now home to tens of thousands of soldiers.

I passed the floor-to-ceiling pillars and walked

along a long arcade, past bathrooms with fake gold, and into the Joint Operations Center. The JOC was housed in an immense, ornate ballroom with high ceilings and gaudy chandeliers. This was the so-called brain center of the war, where representatives of every fighting and supporting unit sat for twelve-hour shifts, day and night, trying to figure out how they were supporting the war effort.

Our desks all faced west. They were arranged in a semicircle, each row constructed higher than the one in front. Lanes ran from the two main doors to steps that went to the top row, and between two pairs of double doors at the front of the room were two enormous sets of screens. Each set was the size of a small-town movie theater and made up of nine smaller screens—a different channel playing on each. On the right there were news channels like Fox, CNN, and Al Jazeera. On the left were live feeds from unmanned aerial vehicles that showed us in real time the raids that were taking place throughout the country.

The logistics units sat in the first few rows of desks. Representatives from the divisions actually fighting the war were seated in the middle rows. I was in the very back row, center, with a view of the whole setup.

The colonels' seats were, during the day shift, occupied by a set of real colonels and generals, but Lieutenant Colonel Johns had those seats all to himself during the night shift. He was surrounded by phones and computer monitors and had a microphone with a placard in front that read "commander." He used it to announce his nightly dictums.

Taking my seat I phoned down to Gus, who worked at a desk in the row below me.

"How's he been so far?" I asked.

"Johns? Oh, he's great. For some reason he has us rewriting our night shift briefs before 0200."

"Because he can," I said.

"Dinner?" Gus asked.

"Yeah, let me figure out what I have to do on my slides and we can grab Wild Bill," I said and hung up.

I sat down and leaned back heavily in my chair. I opened the notes about tonight's assignment from Johns and read enough to get frustrated. I called

Bill, my roommate at Victory who worked the night shift for another unit on the base. I opened the slides I needed to work on but couldn't deal with the demanded changes, so I picked up the phone and dialed Gus again.

"Captain Jeffries," Gus answered.

"Dude."

"I know, it's ridiculous," Gus said.

"He wants me to redo my entire presentation, but everything he suggested was about the aesthetics," I said.

"We all got the same one. Fonts, and point sizes, and bullet formats. He knows we are in Baghdad, right?" Gus said. "He said we couldn't leave our seats until we were done unless it was an emergency."

"This is crazy," I said.

"Wild Bill go to dinner?" he asked.

"Yeah, I told him we're hanging tight."

"Sounds good."

"Alright, man," I said, and Gus hung up the phone.

I pulled up my slides again, but wasn't able to concentrate. Johns was always pulling something like this. He loved feeling like he was a part of the war effort.

My phone rang. "Lieutenant Hendricks," I said.

It was Gus. "The pride of your state is up on Fox News," he said.

"What is it?" I said, holding my headphones over one ear.

"This is Burning Man," Gus said.

"Nevada is home to all kinds of cultural atrocities far worse than Burning Man."

"You mean the whorehouses?" Gus asked.

"No, I'm not even talking about the gambling and the whorehouses. Vegas has Celine. Reno had a Rod Stewart impersonator for years when I was growing up. These are the things we will be remembered for, not a weeklong frat party in the desert."

"I thought you'd like it," Gus said.

"Sorry."

"All good. Okay, out here," Gus said, hanging up.

I turned up the volume on my headphones to hear Fox do its version of in-depth reporting on Burning Man. When I was growing up in Reno in the 1990s, I knew plenty of people who devoted themselves to going every year, but I never went. But I had been reading Brian Doherty's book *This Is Burning Man* over the last few weeks during my shift. Doherty was a fan, but he also appreciated the debate between Burning Man purists and the partiers. I'd probably never end up going. After two years in Baghdad, I'd enjoyed enough good times covered in dust and surrounded by people I didn't like.

Footage of the festival from a helicopter showed the Black Rock Desert floor with the enormous semicircle of campsites all facing the Man in the center. The broadcast showed a diagram of the encampment and its curved, parallel roads running in large semicircles, each with globally relevant names like "Destiny" and "Hope" and "Baghdad," which was a little cloying during the third year of the war, while the roads that ran from the circle's center like spokes were named for the hour of the clock. At the very center, of course, the Man that would burn to the crowd's roar.

"Attention in the JOC, attention in the JOC," I heard Johns saying over the PA system. I took off my headphones and passed a glance to Gus, who was already smirking back at me. "We have approximately three hours before 0200 when we will complete the mission overhaul regarding your daily presentations. Hopefully you have chosen a phased course of action, and will begin working on the finishing touches here in the next two hours," Johns boomed.

"Captain Jeffries," Gus answered.

"Can you believe this?" I muttered.

"I'll get back to you as soon as I know anything, sir," Gus said. "Yes sir, out here." He was wise to fake the call; his boss standing right behind him looking over his slides.

Johns was still droning on, saying nothing of consequence. I looked at the screens on the left and watched UAV footage of a special forces team moving in on an objective somewhere nearby in Baghdad. Johns was asking for everyone to provide him with an individualized update over the PA system starting at the front right corner. This was going to take hours, I thought.

I pulled my microphone down as far as it would

go, turned it on, and flicked the foam rubber over the microphone hard with my middle finger. It sent a loud thump throughout the ballroom, interrupting Johns. I did it again a few seconds later, which elicited a reprimand from Johns to the whole room. Waiting a minute, I pinched the microphone with my fingers and twisted it around almost a full rotation, making the sound of a slowly swinging door in a haunted house. This time there was a quiet laughter from the room and an angrier rebuke from Johns telling us all to make sure our microphones were "in the off position." The faceless night-shifters obliged, clicking their microphones on and off again, creating another storm of pops and crackles, making Johns wait even longer.

Over the next hour, everyone in the JOC seemed focused on updating their slides. I went down to Gus's desk, pretending to help him with his slides— one of two reasons Johns could come up with for these grown men and women to be out of their seats during his "mission overhaul exercise." Gus's were ready, so the two of us joked quietly until I went to the bathroom—the other legitimate reason for grown men and women to leave their seats. When I walked back into the room, two logistics representatives were sitting at the commander's console with Johns, going over printouts of their slides one at a time. Johns was using his red pencil on them.

"Transpo, this is JOC Officer in Charge," Johns said when logistics left. "Come to my position, over," he added to the group of sergeants seated ten feet away from him. I started reading *This Is Burning Man* again, before heading back to my room to sleep until the next twelve-hour shift would start.

I dreaded Johns and my shift when I walked back to the JOC the next night. I crisscrossed the roads in the grid system that made up the living quarters of the camp and passed by the mess hall before walking to the footbridge to the palace. Tonight was going to be just like every other night.

My conversation with Leo was the usual. He laughed about how obnoxious Johns was again, talking about how combat troops were rolling out into Baghdad at that very moment, while Leo, Johns said, took his sweet-ass time checking IDs. Leo said he had to run Johns's ID three times because, damnedest thing, the machine just wasn't working. I walked up to my desk and my phone was already ringing.

"Lieutenant Hendricks," I answered.

"What's up, man?" Gus said.

"Same old, you?" I said.

"I've got something for you," he said. "Let's go walk."

We both hung up and walked down separate aisles to the foyer. Gus was standing there smiling when I shook his hand, and he handed me a list of five telephone numbers.

"What's this?" I asked.

"The number to all five phones at Johns's station," Gus said. "I copied them down last night."

"Is there any sort of caller ID or anything?" I asked.

"I don't think it's possible," he said. "They are DSN, hardwired to an actual switchboard in the camp somewhere. Maybe they could trace it, but why? There's a war going on."

"Is this my copy?" I asked.

"Yeah, I copied it down for you," Gus said.

"What should we do?"

"I think we just play it by ear," he said. "He's going to get talking tonight and one of us should just give him a call."

"Can I do it?" I asked.

"I think you should have that honor," Gus said.

"Thanks," I said, and we took the same stairs back to our seats.

"Pride of Nevada is back on Fox," Gus said as we went to our seats. We both put on our headphones and watched the second episode of the special. Tonight there was a piece on one guy who opened an old speakeasy on the playa, a story about a school bus converted into a replica of the USS Abraham Lincoln, complete with an enormous "MISSION ACCOMPLISHED" banner, and countless images of girls wearing furry boots, bikinis, and a thin layer of dust. I plugged my headphones in just in time for the reporter's closing comments: "for just over a week every year, Black Rock City becomes the sixth biggest city in the state of Nevada. Over the last few years, it has grown into the largest temporary and intentional community in the world."

"They forgot Camp Victory," I said to Gus when he answered his phone.

"Who did?" he asked.

"Camp Victory is the largest intentional community in the world, not Burning Man," I said.

"This is Burning Man," Gus said.

"This is *not* Burning Man," I responded and hung up.

Johns would eventually decide what he wanted to start talking about in an hour, so I settled in and read my book.

I saw Bill's number as my phone rang, and he asked if we wanted to grab midnight chow before I could even answer. I told him I would bring Gus. I was pretending to be busy while scanning my book, and it wasn't long before Johns began talking again. It was time for the nightly changeover briefing, and every station reported on major events since the previous briefing.

It was obvious that Johns was very proud of the changes to the slides he had midwifed the night before, claiming that several of the generals had commented on the changes. At first, Johns's self-importance just annoyed me, but it festered with every additional word that he piled on. In the middle of the next sentence, a self-congratulatory pronouncement on the importance of professionalism in military presentations, the phone on the desk in front of him rang, forcing him to order everyone in the ops center to "standby" while he answered the commander's phone. "Lieutenant Colonel Johns, JOC Officer in Charge, this is a secure line, over," he said, long after I had already hung up the phone. Johns repeated himself, then hung up.

"Guess they didn't know they were calling the three star," he said. "As I was saying, the general was exceedingly pleased with the attention to detail and professionalism exhibited in your presentation this morning and he wanted to pass along his thanks for your work. Standby," he said, this time fielding a phone call from Gus that was disconnected by the time he answered. The quiet chuckle in the room made me uneasy, and the way Johns slammed the receiver down made its point.

Later, we walked out the huge double doors,

into the marbled foyer, over the bridge to the compound's exit and on our way to Bill's compound. Gus and I were taking turns impersonating Johns answering the phones and we were wheezing with laughter by the time we reached Bill. He shared our hatred for Johns, and laughed at our reenactment on our way to the mess hall.

"How did you get the numbers?" Bill asked.

"This guy," I said pointing to Gus, "had the attention to detail to write them down last night while Johns was personally briefing him on the importance of a professional briefing style."

"You did give me the idea by broadcasting the sound of foam rubber over a hot mic while he was talking," Gus said. "I thought I was going to die."

I told Bill about the colonel who tripped over the bottom stair, dumping about four large file folders full of paperwork all over the landing. Gus told him about the new sergeant from the Fourth Infantry Division who openly slept at his desk, mouth wide open, until his own snoring woke him up every night.

The next three nights were almost identical. I chatted with Leo at the guard shack, I read my book while we did our slides, Gus and I watched the Burning Man special, and we conducted coordinated assaults on Johns during his prepared remarks, calling a phone all the way to his right followed by another all the way to his left as soon as he had hung it up. It was becoming obvious that he believed we were behind it. It was also obvious, we told Bill the third night at dinner, that everyone else in the JOC thought it was hilarious. For all of Johns's self-important talk and complicated patter, he proved incapable of keeping a few smart-ass officers in line.

"He's got to know it's us by now," I said, eating a piece of baked chicken.

"How could he prove it, though?" Bill asked.

"I still don't think they would trace the calls, or whatever," Gus said.

"I think that we clearly have two options here," I said. "We can either call it or we can go all in."

"I think it's still pretty funny," Gus said.

"It's hilarious," I said. "We have to escalate."

"But how do you escalate?" Gus asked. "I mean, we've been beating this guy up all week and he hasn't made a real move for us to work with."

"What if we buy a disposable phone from the PX and hide it under some papers or something," Bill suggested.

"It's outside the box," I responded. "But the beauty of it is in its simplicity."

"What if we get away from the phones," Bill said. "You want to lock him in his trailer tomorrow when he's sleeping?"

"That would be awesome," I said. "He's always starting the briefing right as the Burning Man story is getting good."

"I thought you hated that stuff," Gus said.

"I'm even surprising myself," I replied. "What if I just put my headphones on the mic and broadcast the Burning Man report for as long as I can?"

"That's pretty bold," Bill said.

"It's pretty stupid, too" Gus added, laughing.

"But it's not that different from the phones. I mean, from my seat in there, I can see everything. So long as I can keep a straight face, no one will know it's me."

"I don't really have any skin in the game," Bill said.

"Same here," Gus said. "It'll throw him a curve-ball."

When we got back, we learned that Johns had changed the terms of the fight. Right before he began his remarks, two soldiers that worked for him walked up the stairs and settled in as sentries in the back of the room. They tried to look nonchalant, but it was obvious that one was watching me and the other watching Gus. I called Bill and gave him all of the phone numbers and the briefing timeline.

"MND-B," Johns said, referring to the representative in the JOC from Multi-National Division Baghdad, "Your AO has seen extensive enemy contact in the last twenty-four hours. There seem to be two possible scenarios. This is either a sustained, coordinated assault, or multiple, uncoordinated factions acting independently but synergistically. What say you?"

"Sir," the captain covering the night shift for MND-Baghdad said, stalling—he was nowhere near any of the intel sources he would need to answer. "We see no signs of coordinated attacks in our SITREPS from our battalions."

"That's disappointing," Johns responded quickly. "I have several intelligence reports right here in front of me suggesting that what we are seeing is a groundswell of coordinated activity happening throughout your sector, especially in impoverished Shi'ia neighborhoods."

"Sir, relying on the situation reports that have been appropriately declassified for these reports, all I can say is that I can see no patterns or analysis suggesting that the attacks are coordinated," the captain responded.

"I am not dissuaded by your reliance on unclassified reports," Johns responded. "Quite frankly, I remain disappointed that your own analysis, even from open sources, has not arrived at the conclusion that Baghdad is under assault tonight, and something is behind that assault. I would even accept a well-considered argument suggesting that it was not the result of coordinating insurgent activity, but I only hear from you that you do not know because you cannot know, and that that should simply be enough to quell my questions and concerns."

Johns was just warming up, reestablishing

dominance in the room that mocked him, when Bill's call came through. He took a full three seconds before turning around to check with his sentries. His eyes cut to Gus and me before turning back around in his seat to answer his phone. He had no sooner answered when the phone to his far right rang. A phone to his left rang next, and he was walking toward it when the commander's phone rang. Bill must have been using several phones, because several of the phones started ringing at once.

I noticed for the first time that the ringtones for at least two of the phones were different, which made for a surreal melodic affect. Added to it were the laughs of a hundred night shifters who no longer felt the need to keep it in.

Johns was trying to figure out how to turn the ringers off, and for a moment it looked like he was going to call for help from his sentries, but he didn't. Instead, he walked to the phone on his far right and unplugged it, repeating it on all of the phones until the ringing ceased.

"Attention in the JOC! Attention in the JOC!"

he called out in a command voice from the general's center seat, eschewing the microphone for the first time since I had been there. He was standing ramrod straight, fists balled at his side. He repeated his command, louder this time, until everyone in the room was silent and standing at attention, too.

"I realize that it does not feel like we are contributing to the war effort here," he said, loudly, but composed. "Just like you, every time I walk through these doors I have to remind myself that we are at war. And every time I walk through these doors I commit to finding new ways of making sure that you are engaged as well."

Johns took a long breath and looked around the silent room. "Clearly I have failed in my mission," he said, lowering his voice for the first time. "Clearly I have failed to inspire you to care about what is going on with our fellow soldiers, sailors, airmen, and marines throughout Iraq tonight. Clearly I have failed to convey that this is the operations center for the highest headquarters in Iraq and not a college house party."

"Ladies and gentlemen," he said, pointing

toward the screens behind him. "On this screen here you can watch as Army Rangers conduct a raid on the home of a terrorist subject in Baghdad, a city that is currently under attack by the insurgency. They will terrify the civilians who happen to live there, they will kill those who fight back, and some might die. If you think you shouldn't do everything you can to support them, then please leave now. Leave now and do not come back into my operations center."

He turned on his heels and shuffled down the carpeted stairs out the double doors. A senior sergeant put the room at ease when he was gone, but the room remained quiet. I felt my face cool as the blood left it when I sat back down. I watched as the two sentries walked to the colonel's seat and started plugging the silent phones back in.

7

Soldier's Cross

THE PLATOON LEADER sat in the front right seat of his Humvee, still tasting the watery eggs he'd had a few hours before and feeling the sleep in his eyes and the sweat gathering under his uniform. They'd been out on patrol since before dawn, and in the darkness his driver had been getting bogged down in the trenches of human waste that ran through this village. Now that the sun was just coming up his driver could avoid the open sewage, but they could also see the endless trash that filled the streets: product containers, discarded clothing, food waste. Anything that was unwanted inside the Iraqi houses of Tahrir got thrown right outside.

They'd been looking for trouble and finding none. Just as his four Humvees were about to finish serpentining through their last neighborhood, he received a FRAGO, the dreaded call from battalion telling them that they were going to have another mission. They were to go to the local Sunni mosque and see what they could glean from the daily call to prayer. The imam's daily prayers were key sources of communication in the largely illiterate and disconnected local community, but a fragmentary order changing his mission drastically pissed him off. No one could anticipate what a FRAGO was going to look like ahead of time, but he momentarily reveled in the fact that his bosses at battalion had been wrong in denying him the use of one of the battalion's Iraqi interpreters for his morning patrol. He'd long since learned not to argue, though, even after a recent FRAGO had left the battalion staff so confused that another platoon wound up abandoned and pinned down, losing two young soldiers.

"Hey Mac," he said in a quiet morning tone to the young soldier who was filling in as his driver for just this patrol.

"Yessir," Mac responded.

"Those black trenches in the street? You know what they are full of, right?"

"Yessir."

"Then can you pull away from this one over here so I don't have to swim through it to get out, please?"

"Sorry, sir," Mac responded nervously, and slowly moved the vehicle forward.

"It's no big deal, Mac," he laughed, trying to give Specialist McPherson a break. "Valdez does that to me on purpose all the time. I just figure I can train you a little bit since you are new to the job." He popped Mac lightly with the back of his hand to make sure he knew he wasn't in trouble. "Just pull right over there so we can see the mosque and hear the speakers, please." Over the platoon radio he told his men to set up security, get pointed down roads and alleys in all four directions, and settle in for the prayers they'd been ordered to monitor without an interpreter.

Just days before, he had been in his native Las Vegas on R&R. It was a trip that he never thought would arrive and that seemed to be over in an instant. He'd let his soldiers get back home first, waiting so long for his own return that now he only had two months to go in his deployment.

When he was growing up in Las Vegas he avoided the Strip at all costs and laughed at the weekend warriors who rolled through McCarran elated, energized, and high-fiving only to leave three days later bloodshot, spent, and haggard. But with his friends waiting for him, and plenty of arrangements made in advance, this time he had been the one rolling through the airport, and he'd be staying much longer than most out-of-towners.

He only seemed to be awake at night when he was in Las Vegas. There was the night when his friends rented an airport shuttle to carry them from place to place, having more fun than they should, and admitting as much to themselves. There were nights when all his friends had to work the next day, forcing him to go out on his own. The results were always the same: waking up hungover and a bit angry, a slight tremor in his hands from the drinking and the smoking and the dehydration. But then he could sleep the day away and not have to worry about writing incident reports or chasing any FRAGOs.

For nearly all his deployment in Iraq, swimming

pools had been the object of his daydreams. His friend had a pool at home and one night after they had gone out to the Strip and met some Canadian girls, he found himself by that pool with Samantha, a nineteen-year-old from Vancouver, watching the sun come up over the valley. Then they stripped and slipped into the water together. He knew that never would have happened when he simply lived there.

In Iraq now, the sun was coming up through the cloud and smog. The call to prayer seemed to be starting the same, slow and subdued, probably heavy on the praise to Allah and light on the call for jihad. As the sun crested the horizon completely, finally powerful enough to burn through the morning haze, the imam's service became increasingly intense in rhythm, with yelling in response.

"So what are we going to do, sir?" his platoon sergeant asked.

"What's that?" he asked, removing an earplug from his right ear.

"What are we going to do here?"

"We're going to sit here for a while. It's just going

to be one of those mornings," he said, not allowing himself to say what everyone was thinking. "What do you think we're going to hear, Mac?" he asked the driver.

"I'm guessing that we hear how great God is, and how it will all be done if it is God's will. If we listen closely enough, sir," Mac said, referring to Allahu Akbar and inshallah, the only two Arabic phrases that nearly all Americans could hear and understand, if they listened closely.

"You're probably right," the platoon leader said, laughing. "They'll all be reminded that they are a religion of peace, then be ordered to kill all Americans."

"What the hell are we doing here, sir?" his second squad leader asked, walking up from his vehicle in the rear.

"We're listening to the mosque, sergeant. Following orders," he responded, smiling.

"Can't we follow orders better in the shade?" the squad leader asked, using his need to spit a wad of brown saliva as an opportunity to break eye contact from the man whose authority he was challenging.

"Or back on base where we don't have to smell these trenches?"

"Sergeant, I kind of see this as the devil we know. Battalion thought it was a brilliant idea to send us out here to listen to the morning prayers without an interpreter. I think that this is far less inconvenient than going back into the chute for whatever great idea pops up next. I mean, we're already dressed." He was going to go on, but he knew better. He knew that it was his job to relay the orders and shield his men from the chickenshit as best he could, not to prove to his men that he understood and even shared their collective grievance.

"And besides, listen to this guy get down," the platoon sergeant said, eager to change the subject away from his platoon leader's insubordinate remarks about headquarters.

"What is going *on* in there?" Mac asked.

"I'm not so worried about what's going on in there, look at what's going on out here," the squad leader said, squinting under the sun.

"Looks like hajji is actually answering the call to prayer this morning," Mac said as several dozen locals passed in front of them heading toward the mosque. "Is it some sort of hajji holiday?"

"No one told me anything," the platoon leader muttered, staring at the small crowd entering the mosque. He made a report to battalion, letting them know what was going on around them: the gradually intensifying call to prayer, the growing number of adherents entering the mosque from the community, and his current position. "I wonder if they'll let me go in there with them," he said to no one in particular.

"Who? The Iraqis or battalion?" the platoon sergeant asked, still leaning against his platoon leader's vehicle and not taking his eyes off of the front door of the mosque. "I'm not sure the Iraqis could stop you from going in with all of us out here, but we can't go in their mosques unless we are directly engaged by them," he said, answering his own question.

"I'm a Muslim," the platoon leader said nonchalantly.

"What?" the squad leader asked incredulously.

"My dog tags list my faith as Muslim," the platoon

leader said, still not breaking his stare.

"Really?" Mac asked with even more disbelief in his voice than the squad leader.

The platoon leader nodded, still trying to figure out what was going on around them and why there had been dozens of "military-age Muslim males" staring him down as they entered the mosque a few yards away from his Humvee.

"I had no idea," Mac said, as if he was calculating the cost of all the offensive remarks he had made in front of his platoon leader about his faith.

"I'm not really a Muslim, Mac," he said, snapping out of his stare and keying the radio mic to talk to his other vehicles. "Let's try not to interrupt their morning prayer here, but let's dismount teams and get vehicles pointed down these alleyways," he told his guys. "Sergeants?" he said with a raised eyebrow, sending two of his senior NCOs back to execute the order he had just given.

"I still don't get the dog tags, sir," the squad leader said while the platoon leader got out of his vehicle.

"They wouldn't let me put 'Nevadan' on them

when we were getting ready to come over here," he said, dismissing the squad leader as well as the long and personally frustrating process that had ended with him simply choosing to make a particularly timely joke about the "religious faith" line on his dog tag processing form.

"I have no idea what that means," the squad leader said, looking directly at the platoon leader, half distrustful and half confused.

The platoon leader couldn't tell if he was truly puzzled, offended, or just trying to delay getting his squad in position, but he could tell that he wasn't getting off the hook. "At out-processing, during the pre-deployment stuff. I didn't want to fill out the 'religious faith' line on the form. I tried to leave it blank and they wouldn't let me. I tried to write in 'Nevadan' on there, you know, as a joke, but the sergeant didn't think that was funny either. Finally, he handed me off to one of his fellow NCOs who didn't care what I put as long as it was on his list. 'Muslim' was on the list, so I chose it. Now, get to work," he said. "Mac, get pointed down that alley there and watch our front."

"Does your dog tag really say that you are Muslim, sir?" Mac asked.

"Yes," he said, mildly exasperated. He pulled the chain out of his pocket to answer the question for good.

"You know that if you die, they are going to give you Muslim last rites, don't you, sir," Mac said. "That's how the chaplain knows."

"Do you believe in God, Mac?"

Mac pulled out his own dog tags and held them out to show the "Roman Catholic" written across the bottom.

"What's that?" he asked, pointing to a medallion on Mac's dog tag chain.

"It's a medallion appealing to Saint Rose of Lima," he replied. "Sometimes I think it's the only thing that's kept me alive."

"Well then, I think you're superstitious enough for the both of us, Mac," he said laughing. "Be sure and tell the chaplain to get behind cover if you see him leaning over me during a firefight one of these days."

Back in Vegas, the week before, his mom hadn't

handled the same conversation as well as Mac had. She'd seen the dog tags on the kitchen table while he was in the shower and looked like a wounded animal when he came down later for dinner.

"You know, you're just like your father," she said after he tried to explain the joke.

"You mean, I'm a heavy-handed moralist who's into younger women?" he responded quickly, meaning it as a joke.

"That's not funny," his mother said blankly.

He could tell that she wanted to say more, to offer up some explanation for why his father had waited until his son was off at war to have his midlife crisis. It wasn't exactly what he had grown to expect from the man who wouldn't even let his small family have a television because he didn't want to let the evils of the world into his home.

He waited for her to speak but she didn't. He knew that his mother wanted to talk about it. He knew that she almost certainly could not have figured out a way to work through it all by herself. He hadn't yet, but he also knew that he was only home for two weeks. When he thought about it, he hated himself for avoiding the issue. And when his mom told him he favored his father, he hated himself even more.

"How are you doing with all of it, Momma?" he asked seriously for the first time since he'd been home.

"I'm still pretty confused, Michael," she said, "but I'm fine. I don't think any of us saw it coming, but I guess worse stuff happens to people all the time." She was staring past him now, but he could tell that the anger he had heard on the phone months before had started to subside. "I'm still hopeful. I think maybe he was reacting harshly to your leaving, and that this was his only way of dealing with it. He returned one of my calls the other day."

He was momentarily furious that it had become his fault, but he put it all aside and hugged his mother. There was no way his father was coming back, right? Everything he had lived for was a lie, and coming back groveling would take more humility than the man had ever shown. No, he'd moved on, and his son was going to deal with it all later.

"I'm going to head out for a bit, Mom," he said, kissing her on the forehead.

"I wish you'd get your dog tags fixed," she'd said before letting go of his hand.

"It's just a joke, Mom," he'd said, smiling half-heartedly as he left the room.

Hopefully Mac knew it was a joke too. He slapped him on the shoulder, and pointed at the alley closest to their position. "Keep an eye down this alley, and use the wall for cover." The call to prayer seemed to be over now, but there were still rants coming from the speaker. It was a different voice, and although it was louder, he couldn't tell if it was more radical than before. They were to respect the call to prayer and other cultural customs, though nothing about four armed and armored Humvees sitting outside your front door seemed respectful. He wanted to leave. It was a lose-lose, he thought, but he wasn't in control. He picked up the battalion radio mic. "What would you like us to do? Over."

"Stay in position," he heard in response. It wasn't what he wanted to hear, but he didn't have many options.

"We're going to sit tight for a while, boys," he said into his platoon mic. "The idiots at battalion are trying to figure out how to tell us we shouldn't be here without having to say that they shouldn't have sent us here. Shouldn't be long now."

"Yeah, no time at all," a voice came back over the radio.

* * *

HIS PLATOON was in a good security position when they started to hear shooting.

"Please tell me those shots are coming from inside the mosque," his second squad leader said over the radio, laughing. "I kind of want to see what the inside of one of those things looks like."

"Could you imagine the bloodbath if we went in there?" the platoon leader responded. The shots were now sporadic, and it became increasingly clear that they were coming from a block or two north of their position. They weren't hitting anywhere near them, but they were definitely being fired on from nearby.

"Get back behind that wall, Mac," he yelled, leaving the radios alone to see when and how the shooting was going to stop. Mac's alley was only a few feet wide, not even wide enough for a vehicle, and Mac covered it prone. He was a right-handed shooter, and the position his platoon leader had given him to cover was also on his right, forcing him to expose more of his body in order to cover the alley. "Switch sides. I think you've got better cover from this side of the alley."

"Are you serious, sir?" Mac said, looking up at him more confused than when he had been told his boss was a Muslim. "There's a trench there."

"Well," the platoon leader said. "Don't swim in it. But you've got to get better cover than that wall. You're hanging half your body out into that alley." Once Mac was in position, the platoon leader squatted down behind him, pressed against the wall, relying on the other man's eyes for what was happening in the alley.

The shooting seemed to be building, but it still wasn't much more than harassment fire. The imam was still yelling loudly and fiercely, building to rhythms that the platoon leader had only heard during Ramadan before he went on leave. The platoon leader looked up when the imam's words became more staccato, seeming to match the random shots coming from enemy AK47s popping in the alleyways near the platoon.

"It's hot out here, isn't it, Mac?" he asked.

Before Mac could answer, the imam was yelling again, perhaps signaling the fighters to match his words with their actions, and they did. For the first time since the shooting started, they could see enemy maneuvering, streaming out of the far side of the mosque and trying to flank the stationary platoon through the alleys to their east and west. The platoon's vehicle gunners were well positioned, and the intensifying fire sparked off a vicious response from their machine guns. The platoon leader reached his radio and called battalion for backup.

His men had already killed a group of poorly organized and blindly assaulting insurgents. He was confident. His men had done this before, dozens of times, and very well. They had superior firepower, superior skill, and superior communication. He didn't wait to hear battalion's response before checking on his squads. He gave a thumbs-up to his nearest squad leader, and got two in return. He got the same from his other squad leader and his platoon sergeant at the end of their position.

"I think this ought to be over pretty soon, Mac," the platoon leader yelled once he got back to the wall. "The shooting is dying down."

"What?" Mac yelled back.

"I think it's dying down," he said again.

"It sure sounds that way," Mac yelled, still sprawled out and prone, peering down the alleyway.

"Did you shoot at all?"

"A little," Mac yelled, still concentrating on his alley. "You think they planned this attack, sir, or do you think we pissed them off because we were here during their prayers?"

"I think that the morons in charge still think this is the Cold War they grew up with. I don't think they have a clue, and they wound up putting us in the wrong place at the wrong time," he answered.

"Do they do that a lot?" Mac asked, staring down the sights of his rifle. "I mean, are most of our missions this—"

Their alley, the alley that had been the quietest avenue of approach for the enemy since the shooting started, erupted into a torrent of fire, dust popped at their feet and bullet holes appeared in the mud and brick walls around them. He tucked his head while the shooting got closer.

"You good, Mac?" he yelled over the fire, seemingly paralyzed by the rapid metallic clacking of the nearby AK47s. "Mac, are you good?" he asked again, enunciating each word as loudly as he could. He didn't look down at Mac. "Mac, get up," he ordered. Finally he looked down, the concentrated fire still suppressing his position. Mac was fully slouched, his rifle was toppled under his weight. The growing pool of blood coming out of his forehead was already mixing with the black pool of human waste in the trench next to them. "Mac, get up," he yelled once more.

He grabbed Mac by his vest near his shoulders and rolled him onto his back. Evaluate the casualty like you've been trained a thousand times, he told himself. There was no responsiveness when he called his name. He wasn't breathing and there was blood streaming from his head. Everything else he was supposed to check for—the burns, the broken bones, the shock—were all irrelevant. "You're going to be okay, Mac," he said in a voice that he knew he couldn't expect Mac to believe.

LATER THAT AFTERNOON he was back in his room, still sweating and filthy, sitting in a camping chair that was nearly as broken as he was. He was thinking about how he said goodbye to his mom when he left Vegas. They hadn't had any more conversations that mattered for the rest of his trip. She didn't push him on anything anymore, and he did his best not to flaunt the fun he was having. Their truce had allowed for a few distinctly good nights: a dinner at P. J. Clarke's, a visit to the Springs Preserve, and a movie night like they used to enjoy as a family.

On the last day before going back to Iraq he asked her if she wanted to say her goodbyes at home and let him take a cab to the airport. She allowed for it, but only after putting up a fight. When he walked downstairs in his newly washed uniform, smelling like laundry soap and fabric softener for the first time in months, he could barely look at her sitting at the kitchen table. Her eyes were puffy and she was crying silently into a dish towel, looking like a grieving widow.

"You know I love you, Momma," he said softly, pulling her head into his chest. "You know I'm not leaving because I want to, right?"

"I know that, honey," she whispered between sobs, her throat too swollen from holding back her screams to actually allow her a voice. "I just love you so much."

"I love you too, Momma."

"I know you do," she whispered.

"I'll be home in two months, Momma. Back in Germany. Then I'll be back in Vegas four months later. We just have to hang on."

"You know I can't lose you," she said, mustering all of the strength to hold onto her youngest son's torso and to voice the words they'd both been avoiding. She was heaving now, bawling. "I'm so sorry," she said. "I'm sorry. I know you don't need this, but I can't. I can't." Her body fell limp and she let go of her son. "God, don't take my baby."

"I'll be home, Momma. I'll be home."

His cab arrived shortly after and it was everything he could do to leave. He hadn't mentioned it, but his mother had aged ten years in the year since he'd left. Her hair was grayer and her eyes were more desperate. How much older would she look when he came back next time? How much longer would she last if he didn't? Thinking these things actually offered him solace when he remembered Mac's death. Or maybe it wasn't solace, he thought. Maybe seeing his mother like that just hurt worse.

HE'D HEARD THAT there were already investigations to establish guilt. There were certain to be rumors, too. He had other things that mattered, though, like things he could control. His immediate commander had directed him to have his guys make sure that Mac's personal effects were clear of anything that might be embarrassing when his parents received them, and also to build Mac's cross for the memorial ceremony the following day. As much as he didn't want to move from his chair, he couldn't imagine delegating those tasks to anyone.

Organizing Mac's gear made him realize that although he had been Mac's platoon leader for at least eighteen months, he hadn't really known him at all. He knew that he was an excellent athlete and wanted to coach high school basketball when he got out. He knew that his father was a McPherson and his mother was first-generation American from Peru. And, he knew that Mac was not the best soldier in the platoon, but he was probably the most beloved. There were several extra sets of Mac's dog tags that said he was blood type A positive, that he had the 573 prefix for his California Social Security number, and that he was a Roman Catholic. He smiled when he found a diary with Mac's handwriting across the front: "Specialist McPherson, John Taylor, one each." The phrase was how he often introduced himself into any room or group, a sort of military-issued third person that spoke both to his sense of humor and his willingness to fully accept the identity that the army had given him. In the diary were loving descriptions of his wife and son, who were back in Germany. There was a worn and creased picture tucked between pages to prove it. It said that he was terrified of the war on a daily basis, and had handwritten prayers to his God to prove that, too.

The Soldier's Cross is a makeshift memorial for soldiers killed in battle. It has a four-foot plywood cube as a base. Mac's boots were filled with sand and laced up until they stood centered on the plywood as rigid as they did when he wore them. His rifle, with bayonet fixed, was sticking out of a hole in the top of the box behind the boots with the butt-stock pointed straight up. The platoon leader used a toothbrush and soap to make sure the helmet was cleaned of blood and bone before resting it, canted slightly forward on the stock of the rifle, sitting just over the dog tags that hung around the middle of the rifle.

He could imagine it standing in the middle of the gravel lot in front of headquarters with the companies formed up around it. The company's first sergeant would stand at the podium in front of the formation and conduct a symbolic final roll call while the men stood at attention. When no answer returned from McPherson's empty spot in the formation, it would be turned over to the battalion commander, who, he imagined, would talk about how all of this could have been averted. He'd probably even call the fallen soldier John, as if he knew Mac and had forgiven him the difference in rank.

The platoon leader was struck by how impersonal the cross was. It looked just like every other one that had to be built over their time in Iraq, just like the one someone would have built for him if things had gone differently. The small Saint Rose of Lima medallion might have been the only thing that would have distinguished Mac's cross from his own if he hadn't been instructed to remove it.

8

Watching Him Die

"DID YOU SAY LEAVE HIM HERE?" I asked into the radio handset. I was pressing it against my ear as hard as could and covering my left ear too, but I still couldn't hear anything. It wasn't that loud because the fighting had moved a few blocks north. Maybe the radio signal was weak.

"Did you say leave him here? Over," I said, louder this time.

"Yeah, roger," came an answer. "Just strap him down to something so he can't leave and we'll just—" the signal filling with a high-pitched squeal before I could yank it away from my ear. My orders were to move northwest a few blocks and join the other platoon in a skirmish that I could hear was already winding down. The wounded prisoner we were to leave behind.

My platoon was where we had made initial

contact earlier in the afternoon. We'd been here for hours now, my men pulling security behind garbage piles with dead men—only a few and none mine—scattered in positions that wouldn't have been humanly possible a few hours before.

Then there was the lone survivor from the group we'd engaged, a jihadi who was badly wounded and barely hanging on. He was slouching against a gate with his bloody legs splayed out in front of him and his arms at his sides. A bullet had grazed his left side, opening up a deep cut nearly six inches. His skin was graying and he'd stopped praying.

"Harrison!" I shouted for the gunner on my vehicle.

"Sir," Harrison said, coming over at a tired clip.

"Zip him to that gate," I said. "Nothing terrible, just keep him here so they can send an evac vehicle out to carry him in later." The dying man's leg flinched as soon as I was done giving the order. "Get Valdez to keep a barrel in his face while you're at it," I added.

"I'd hate to see this prick bleed to death," Harrison said, motioning for Valdez to come over.

"Let me know when you are done," I said, walking back to my radios to get a report from my roommate, who was the platoon leader wrapping up the fight northwest of us. Our platoons were close and the signal was strong enough for me to hold the radio handset to my left ear, which was bad from too much percussion from too many close explosions. The fighting had ceased, he told me, and now they were holding ground and waiting for orders.

"You having trouble with your battalion frequency?" I asked.

"No, I've got them strong, but you're coming in pretty weak on this frequency," he said. "Let me know when you're en route, over."

"Roger that," I said, unsure if he could even hear me. "Let's get everybody mounted up," I yelled, glad that the people I was talking to could hear me for seemingly the first time that whole day.

"Hey, sir, he wanted you to have this," Harrison said, and he slapped a bloody handprint on the front of my pant leg.

"Dick."

"Me or the dead guy?" Harrison asked, dancing

out of the way of my reach and laughing.

"Get up there," I said, giving up the chase and motioning toward the gunner's hatch. "We ready to go?" I asked into the handset on my platoon network. I watched the man's chest rise slowly and slightly and heard Harrison yelling a mocking goodbye to him as we pulled out to meet up with the other platoon.

I remembered that day every time I had to wear those pants. I'd tried to scrub them later that night, but the handprint wouldn't come out. I had only three pairs of tan camouflage pants, meaning every week or so I had to wear that handprint.

There were the good memories from that day, like the first sight of the dead men who had unsuccessfully tried to kill us moments before. There were the bad memories, like helping my roommate carry one of his soldiers with severe gunshot wounds to a truck so he could be evacuated—a task that left me with my own bloody hands. And then there was my memory of the man tied to the gate. He wouldn't just die and make everyone's life easier, and he wasn't alive enough to provide useful

information. He was just there, splayed and graying, strapped to that gate.

I didn't think about him all that often, but I did
as I put on those sweaty, dirty, bloodstained pants
for what was likely my last scheduled patrol as a platoon leader in Iraq. Our last mission was a generic
presence patrol in the northern half of our sector. It was routine. I took the order to my platoon
sergeant and I told him I wanted to take everyone
with us, just to be safe. If anything went bad, I told
him, I didn't want to have to explain to the commander why I left some of the guys back. I was surprised at how hard he pushed back. "No one wants
to be the last one killed in Iraq," he said, and every
time I took them off the base, I increased the risk
of somebody getting killed. I'm sure he was talking
about my guys getting killed, but it also applied to
the Iraqis, I thought.

I wrote the plan for as few of our guys as possible,
but I resented him for challenging me like that, at
least at first. The more I thought about it, though,
the more I realized he was right. Any moment of
any day a disguised bomb could blow you up. Even

in the best circumstances, with the best soldiers and the best training and equipment, you could never be in control of your environment here. You had to accept the routine helplessness of being in Iraq, or ritualize the illusion of control.

I grabbed the sling that held my M4 across my chest and headed toward the door, where my helmet dangled from a hook with my sunglasses and earplugs inside. I grabbed it all at once and lumbered through the doorframe toward my platoon's trucks, just like I had done before every mission for this entire year. The concrete floors and walls trapped the cool of the air conditioners in the hallway, making the first part of the walk pleasant.

When I got to the door that led out into the heat, I set my helmet down, reached over my head with my left hand, and pulled my right ear open by the top. I pushed an earplug into place with my other hand. My right ear was my good ear, better by some 60 percent, leaving me nearly deaf by the time the earplug settled. Even so, for the sake of following orders that seemed ridiculous, I pushed the left earplug into my bad ear, not even caring if it seated properly.

I paused to pack a pinch of chewing tobacco into my lower lip. It was always the last thing I did before walking out, my helmet sitting loose on my head, unstrapped, my sunglasses covering my eyes, and my earplugs blocking out the ubiquitous whir of the camp's generators. The tobacco would make my stomach hurt, but with all of my other senses dampened and muted the pungent taste and smell were at their strongest. I enjoyed this short walk from my room out to my platoon and our trucks more than most things in my day. There was something about coming out of a deep nap, the salty tea brewing in my mouth, and the gravel crunching under my feet and sending a dull echo through my sealed ears.

Once I was there, and once my guys were ready to go, I'd break the suction and pull out the earplugs. Just as I was ordered, I'd remind my soldiers to wear their earplugs, and to buckle their seatbelts, too. They were both unit requirements, and it was my responsibility to make sure that I at least reminded them, making me no better than the bureaucrat who made the decision in the first place.

I didn't really mind the smart-ass responses my

safety reminders always evoked. No one would be stupid enough to wear earplugs and seatbelt on a combat patrol. We took daily trips through a tough city, I had four vehicles to keep together, and I had to manage two radios in my ears all the time. I broke the rules just like they did, but I still had to tell them that earplugs and seatbelts were the standard.

A pebble hit my helmet as I walked the line of trucks. Even with my head down I knew that it was my driver, Valdez, who was mounting a heavy machine gun on top of my truck. Another pebble hit my helmet, but I still didn't look up. Valdez had probably been up for hours already, but there was no way I was going to acknowledge him just yet. Then an oily rag hit me in the face leaving a grease spot on my sunglasses and a gritty mess on my face. Valdez was now standing next to me, laughing. I wiped the oil off my lens and face with my sleeve. Leaning over I spit a mouthful of tobacco juice on Valdez's boot.

I'd carried that spit all the way from my room, just like I had done every day. The first spit was always the most gratifying, and this one also settled a score.

Valdez hopped back onto the hood of the truck and started calling for me again. I looked at my watch, it was still fifteen minutes before we had to leave. I pulled my earplugs out. I could feel the sleep leave my voice when I yelled for my guys to get together for our briefing: mission, location, earplugs, and seatbelts.

"Hey, sir, could you hear what I was playing for you?" Valdez asked, pointing to a battery-powered CD player that was next to him on the truck.

"I didn't," I said, checking if the radio to battalion worked.

"It was your song," Valdez said.

"Everything ready to go?" I asked.

"Yeah, all done, sir," Valdez said, pulling a heavy armored vest over his gangly body.

"What song was it?" I asked, leaning into the passenger compartment to test the radios again.

"He said it was your song, sir. 'Bombs over Douchebags,'" chimed Private Harrison, proud of his joke as he scurried onto the top of the truck.

"What song was it, Valdez?" I asked again.

"It was your Reno song, the country one, but it was by some punk band instead. I thought it would have pissed you off before the mission."

"It always pisses me off to hear anyone cover the Reverend Johnny Cash," I said. "Glad I missed it."

I was from Reno, a fact that amused some in my platoon. To me it was a unique town that never seemed to live down its reputation for casinos, brothels, and wedding chapels in a town famous for divorce. My guys found it much more amusing to reference a popular television show that I would never admit to having seen.

I loved Johnny Cash, and I loved that song. My family was from Tennessee and had moved to Reno right before I was born. My parents and brothers could all legitimately claim to be southern, and I couldn't. I'd always felt like Cash's song gave me a claim both to my roots and the town I grew up in.

After the mission brief, we got into our trucks. I felt a kick to my shoulder as I picked up the radio handsets, but I ignored Harrison's plea for attention. I took one last look at our route on my map, and then another jarring kick hit my shoulder. I ignored it again, but before I could get my helmet strapped, Harrison pushed it off my head and onto my lap with his boot.

"Why is Harrison so immature, V?" I asked.

"It probably has something to do with the fact that we always drive as fast as we can through shit trenches while he's up there," Valdez said through his laughter.

I pointed for him to start moving. "You still got that song?" I asked him. Valdez motioned toward the stereo sitting on the seat behind us. "Let's hear it," I said, figuring on killing the two minutes before our convoy departed. It wasn't as bad as I thought it would be.

"All vehicles on Route 5, heading west," my radio announced. The handset at my right ear gave me a direct line to the three trucks behind me. It always provided information I wanted to hear, from people I wanted to hear from. My left ear received the far less desirable news. It was the battalion headquarters giving me a FRAGO, telling me to extend my mission, or to do something that didn't make any sense. By the time the trucks opened up their engines, the radios I pressed up to my ears were all I could hear. The massive engine in the six-ton vehicle screamed on the open road, and sitting there, for the first time all year, I decided to put my earplugs back in.

The engine and the earplugs stopped everything. I yelled the first part of Cash's song in Valdez's direction, but he couldn't hear me. I yelled the lyrics again, this time with a more serious look on my face. I pointed at the route we were going to take on my map. I bellowed as loud as I could, but the engines were so loud I still couldn't even hear myself. Valdez nodded, acknowledging the route I was still tracing on the map with my finger.

"So we're staying east on Route Blue and then heading south on Route Red?" he asked as we slowed at a checkpoint on the outskirts of the city.

I shrugged, pointing to my earplugs. I made a report to battalion once we cleared the check-point, not sure if they even heard me. After the first checkpoint, we could travel fast for half an hour on this route. Valdez knew what to do. Harrison knew his part. We'd be just fine.

I started humming as loudly as I could as we picked up speed again. I could feel the vibration in my chest and throat, but I still couldn't actually hear anything. I sang the song again, slapping Valdez's arm to the locomotive rhythm while I did it. "But I shot a man in Reno," I yelled as loud as I could, "just to watch him die."

I loved identifying with the coarsest line of that song. I loved that I was in Reno just a few months prior, on leave from Iraq, and I imagined that the town still felt the same as when Cash had written that song. Fifty years after he recorded it I was in Iraq, watching people die all the time—but only watching; even after being a platoon leader for twelve months I hadn't fired my weapon in anger once.

I was proud of that fact when I thought about the deployment in terms of my job as a platoon leader. My job wasn't to be a killer. My job was to keep the handset on my right ear so that I knew where all of my guys were, and to keep the other handset on my left ear so that higher-ups knew where we were and what we needed.

But I was also ashamed of the fact that I'd never fired a shot. I was a platoon leader at war, and it wasn't like there weren't plenty of chances to kill someone, or at least fire off a warning shot. My guys had killed. And they probably quietly judged me for not killing.

In the end, though, I got a pass because killing wasn't really something anyone ever talked about. My guys never talked about it, with me at least, and neither did my peers, not counting the gallows humor that followed every good fight.

"How'd it go?" I'd asked my roommate once after he came back from a firefight.

"Good enough," he said.

"Anybody get hurt?" I asked.

"Just some insurgents, no real people," he said, and we laughed at the paraphrased Tarantino line.

Another time my roommate said, "We were just picking them off one at a time."

"How many were there?" I asked.

"Probably about ten," he said.

"How many did you kill?"

"Probably about twenty."

That was about as deeply as we discussed it.

The pride and the shame were strangely reconciled for me in the end, though: every person that my platoon killed or didn't kill was my responsibility. If they killed the right guy, I would get credit for it from headquarters. If they killed the wrong guy, I would stand a good chance of being formally investigated.

We'd certainly killed the wrong guys. There was the time when we'd set up two checkpoints on one of the city's major highways to allow the bomb squads to detonate the roadside bombs that had been placed along the median. Both groups of the platoon had done everything right on their stretch of road: signs in Arabic telling drivers to stop 150 meters out, cones stretched across the road at 100 meters, and then concertina wire stretched across the road at 50 meters—my guys knew to fire at any car that got as far as that wire. Even with all of these precautions, there were cars that tested us. With my group, a minivan barreled past all of the notices and into the wire before it screeched to a halt. Amazingly, the driver just reversed, turned around, and drove back the way he came, waving apologetically.

When the other half of the platoon faced a car that just wouldn't stop, they were forced to fire, sending the car careening into a tree. By the time I got there, the passenger was out of the car and yelling with glass shards in his neck. The trunk had popped open when the car hit the tree. There was nothing in it. There was nothing in the back seat either. It wasn't a car bomb. The driver had just made a mistake.

"Ooh," Harrison said, smiling when he saw the driver. "He'll be alright."

The machine-gun rounds had hit him near the bridge of the nose and the top-left quarter of his head was gone. Brain and skull chips were everywhere. We pulled him out onto the ground. An ambulance would come for the passenger, who kept yelling.

I wasn't remorseful that day. There was no way to know what was in the car and why it wasn't stopping in its tracks.

"Charlie 1-6, Charlie 1-6, this is Viper 6, over,"

someone said over the battalion radio. I ignored it. Valdez was used to keeping the convoy moving forward as fast as I would let him, and I had no interest in slowing him down today.

We'd also killed the right guys, like the day we left that guy strapped to the fence. That morning had been frenetic. We'd been driving around the city chasing down false reports of enemy activity when we drove north on a street we didn't know. A mosque on our right blared an angry call to prayer and we didn't see the enemy behind a wall on our left. We were moving through an intersection past a school and some houses at about ten miles an hour when Harrison hollered and spun his .50-caliber machine-gun turret toward the wall and fired.

A rocket screamed between my truck and the second truck, and slammed into the mosque. Valdez drove us behind a wall on the street perpendicular to where we had taken fire and turned us around as the other three trucks pulled up fast behind us.

My platoon sergeant dismounted and screamed for Valdez to pull forward. He and several of his soldiers got behind the hood of the huge armored truck and as Valdez slowly advanced the truck they, and Harrison from above, kept firing at the house across the street. They got the three insurgents who had been out in the open firing back and who were now lying in the street. When the shooting stopped, my vehicles moved out into the area where the bodies were strewn.

My platoon shoved out into a circle with the dead men in the middle. If we'd taken out three on one street, I thought, these were not the only ones we'd have to kill. I sent a team into the school. There were two dead inside. From the house across the street came an elderly couple, implausibly smiling from ear to ear and waving.

One of the guys that Harrison shot was gurgling in the middle of the street. He was positioned awkwardly on his arm and he didn't even have the power to untangle his legs. Another was at a ninety-degree angle to him, head-to-head, still alive, too. Their blood mixed in the dirt beneath them, and the pool was growing toward the third body that was crumpled a few feet away, clearly dead. The two who were still alive didn't acknowledge us as we approached.

I walked back around the corner to my truck. Although my ears were weak and ringing, I thought I could sense calm in the air. The situation was secure, and I had to make a report to headquarters. Before I pushed the button on my radio, I heard three quick shots ring out. They were American shots, not AK47. I looked toward the bodies to see one of my sergeants appear, nodding at me with a smile.

It was later that we found the fourth man, who was still inside the gate. One of Harrison's bullets had gone through the wall and ripped open his side. We kicked his gun away and kicked his arm out from under him, sending him to the ground. My medic went to work on his side, trying to stop the bleeding. Then the interpreter went to work on him, too. We weren't going to get anything useful from him and we kicked his arm out from under him again.

Gunshots cracked the air outside, AK47 this time, and we took cover behind whatever was closest to us in the small yard—the brick wall, the palm tree, even the wounded insurgent. I scrambled outside, my head and shoulders below the brick wall. My platoon sergeant was already there. Two second-story windows about a block to the west received the bulk of the fire from Harrison's machine gun. The firing stopped, and the ringing calm came back to my ears. One of my squads used axes to open and search the trunks of three civilian vehicles near our position. We'd search the house we were outside of next. All the while, the wounded man writhed under the palm tree, treated but graying.

We were not attacked for four more hours. We sat baking in the sun next to open garbage pits, sewage trenches, a dying man, and anything else that seemed to get worse with heat and time. Other units maneuvered around us and we were locked in place, securing the intersection, checking on the wounded man, and waiting.

I walked back into the courtyard to see that Harrison was still guarding the graying man. The man's machine gun, a heavy-caliber weapon not unlike some of the smaller guns on the tops of American trucks, was set close to him by Harrison, daring the man to give us a reason to finish him off. Harrison pushed his boot into the wounded man's bloody side. The insurgent only focused on the prayer beads wrapped between his bloody hands.

"How's he making it," I asked Harrison, still not sure what we were going to do with him.

"He seems to like it when you do this," Harrison said, kicking him in the back of the head with the toe of his boot. "Whoopsy," Harrison said, jostling the man's head again with his foot, harder this time.

The man slowly raised his head, resting it back on the palm tree he was leaning against. He looked down, then looked back up at us. He was breathing harder now. His eyes dropped back to his feet and his hands dropped back to his side in one motion.

"He's gonna go for it, isn't he," I asked Harrison while the dying man mustered his strength. "Look how badly he wants to kill you, Harrison. He's as angry as your wife was when you pissed the bed on leave," I said, watching the man's chest rise faster.

"Yeah, but my wife—"

"Here we go," I said as we both lunged toward the wounded man. Harrison was standing on the hand that went for the gun and I jammed the barrel of my rifle into the man's cheekbone.

The insurgent reached over his body with his free hand, but his head was pinned to the tree and his hand was pinned to the ground. I clicked my rifle from "safe" to "fire," and jammed it harder into his face. "You don't really want to do that," I barked quietly through my teeth.

"He's reaching for his weapon, sir," Harrison said gravely, taking his foot off of the limp hand. "How does that not represent a deadly threat?" he asked rhetorically. The man's hands were moving so slowly and weakly that he couldn't get to the gun. He looked down over the barrel that was pressed against his cheek, trying to see how much further he had to reach.

"What are you doing," I said to the wounded man, leaning almost as hard as I could into the buttstock of my rifle. The pressure on his face forced him to give up his pursuit of the weapon at his side, just out of his reach. I stood up and kicked the man's weapon further away, and then walked out of the yard toward my truck.

"You should have done it, sir," Harrison said. "These guys were trying to kill us a few hours ago."

"So you'd rather see him die quickly?" I asked, not sure if I even believed my argument. Harrison didn't answer. "Keep an eye on him."

The order came over the radio. Valdez, who was manning the radios while I was away, sent word that we were to link up with the platoon to the north-west. I picked up the battalion handset and confirmed. The fighting was almost done, but we were going to go hunker down at a traffic circle in the middle of the city and regroup with the other platoons.

I asked about the dying man. There was no way that I was going to volunteer to pack him in one of our already cramped trucks for the rest of the day. It was midday and there was no telling how much longer we would be away from base, and the wounds weren't getting better in time. As bad as the radios were when I asked, the order was clear: zip him and leave him. They said they'd send out a vehicle to get him later, but I knew he would die that day.

THE ROUTE I PLANNED for our last patrol would take us by the village where it all happened that day. Valdez yelled something and pointed ahead. I knew he was asking if we should take the bridge or go through the village, but I just shrugged and pointed to my earplugs. I moved the map that was on my knees and looked at the handprint Harrison put on my pants. I looked at him sitting up there, slouched as low as he could be in the turret of his gunner's hatch, unable to shoot and unable to be shot. No one wanted to be the last one killed in Iraq.

9

The Golden Dragon

FOR THEIR SIX-MONTH anniversary, Amy presented Matt with two framed pictures. The first was a grainy black-and-white photo printed on cheap glossy paper and hastily framed. It was their twenty-week sonogram, which he hadn't been home for. The second was a three-by-five photo of him and his brothers from his high school days taken with a disposable camera. He'd had it laminated and carried it with him for six years of military training, deployments, combat, and even the times he came home to visit his family. She gave them to him outside the Golden Dragon, a favorite Vietnamese restaurant in Reno, where he had taken her for their anniversary. It was also the first real date they had together since he'd left the army the week before.

"How many?" an Asian man asked through a heavy accent from a few tables away as they waited to be seated. Matt had always assumed him to be the owner—he drove the big Mercedes that was usually parked out front—but he worked the cash register and seated guests, too. Matt respected that.

"Just two," Matt mouthed, knowing full well that saying the number wouldn't be heard over the guests anyway.

"It's very busy, sir," the owner said, motioning for them to wait a moment while he cleaned a table.

"We're fine," Matt said, sitting down in an overstuffed booth bench by the front door, regretting it immediately when the next couple opened the entrance up to the frigid evening air before deciding to try somewhere else, opening up the door again to leave.

"There's got to be a way to do that without letting the air in," he said to himself.

"What? Open the door?" Amy laughed, hugging his jacketed arm.

"It's just ridiculous out there," he said.

"It's not that bad," she said, smiling.

"My body is still used to the desert heat, I guess," he said.

"I'm glad you're home, Matthew," she said, wrapping her arms around his larger body and putting her head to his chest.

"It's good to be back," he said, kissing her hair softly and fighting a shiver.

Six months before he was home on leave from Iraq, conflicted about who he was and who he wanted to be when he got out of the army. She was wandering, questioning her parents' religion for the first time. They were both drinking when they met, him hard and practiced and her excitedly. Luckily she remembered his name when he went back to Iraq a few days after their night together. She was glad she had someone to give the sonogram to and glad that he saw it as a gift.

He looked down at the pictures she had given him again, wondering if the baby was a boy or a girl. He loved that she had matted and framed the other one, too. It was a simple picture of a scene his brothers had staged. They and their friends had gone camping in the Big Smoky Valley, about forty-five minutes south of Austin, Nevada, right before he went to basic training. It was his official and final going-away party, his closest friends gathered by his brothers to enjoy everything they couldn't enjoy as eighteen-, nineteen-, twenty-year-olds in Reno—at least not easily.

Matt was resting in a hammock moments before the picture was taken. The South Fork of the Twin River flowed behind him, the hammock tied between two trees. He was probably sleeping off an afternoon hangover in the beautiful shade: listening to nothing, fearing nothing, and wishing for nothing. Or he might have been somewhere between worlds, somewhere between where he was and where he would be, somewhere between all things that mattered in his life and the unknown that would matter more soon.

The shutter on the camera snapped as his oldest brother poured a pitcher of icy water on him in the hammock. His other brother looked on from behind them, not even trying to conceal a smile. He lurched with surprise at the icy water, and the hammock did its best to pitch him onto the ground. You could see his other brother standing beside the tall tree behind the hammock, looking on with a grin that filled his cheeks and nose and eyes while he waited for the eldest's action and the youngest's reaction. It was a grin of quiet commission, the kind that often precedes a solid belly laugh, constrained momentarily and by necessity.

Matt liked his smile in the picture. It was the smile of surprise, the kind that didn't betray an ounce of fury, which would have been more than justified at the moment of shock when the picture was taken. He laughed as hard as or harder than his brothers, and with full appreciation for the plot that would leave him stunned, freezing, and down in the dirt and pine needles of the desert floor.

Looking up from the pictures, he realized that the Golden Dragon was exactly how he had remembered it—cheap, lacquered pictures on the wall, foil address stickers announcing by number the tables where guests were seated, synthetic tabletops, dirty carpet. It was all still there, as was a diversity of customers coming from the area. The building across the street was a weekly motel, much like the ones whores worked in a block away. Kitty corner to the restaurant was a casino. A Catholic hospital

sat a block to the east, with the interstate winding like a prayer ribbon north of it all. Back when
the city planners were trying to bring a university
to the town, they argued to parents that the interstate would separate their kids from the casinos and
the whores on the other side. A footbridge had con-
quered that divide and the unseemly parts of town
had crept all the way up from the south.

The younger generation of the family of immi-
grants who owned and operated the Golden
Dragon traveled the footbridge from their dorm
rooms on campus to work the twenty-five or so
tables at the restaurant. They'd wear their black
uniforms and check right into the constant bus-
tle out of the kitchen, never missing a beat. They'd
speak English to each other, mostly, and switch
effortlessly to their native tongue for their parents and older relatives, and to their cousins who
had joined the family after they had established the
business successfully.

"How are you, sir?" asked the man Matt thought
was the owner.

"Very good, sir. Very good. Thank you."

"Number eight and number twelve?" the owner asked, setting their glasses on the table. Seeing Matt's hesitation, he added, "Or, do you want menus?"

"Oh," Matt said. "Yes, a number eight for me. Amy? A number twelve?"

"That'd be great," she said.

"Thank you," he said, hustling directly back to the door to seat the next set of guests.

"Oh excuse me, sir," Matt said as the owner walked past their table again toward the register. "Can I get spring rolls, too? And for the number eight, can you put the beef on the side, please?"

"Sure," the owner said and walked away to put their order in.

"That's pretty amazing, actually," Matt said after he left. "I haven't been here in a long time and he still remembers that I eat a number eight."

"Especially with as busy as this place is all the time," Amy said. She squeezed a lemon into her water and smiled. "I've been coming here a lot over the last six months. In fact, I was just here last week. Want to guess what I ordered?"

"A number twelve?" he smiled.

"Good guess," she laughed.

He looked at the photo of himself and his brothers while Amy took a drink from her water. There were several reasons he had carried a copy with him all over the world, but the biggest was simply that he loved it. It didn't express any powerful revelations about their relationship at that instant. It didn't show that his older brothers finally respected him. It didn't show that they admired or resented his choice that would take him from them. It just showed them. They were brothers. They pulled pranks. And they laughed about it. Hard. Over beers later that night he had become emotional, asking his brothers not to let him change, but their quiet responses said what they all already knew—that there was no turning back.

"They are open until 3:00 a.m. now," she said, pointing to a homemade banner over the counter behind him.

"Yeah," he said, looking over his shoulder. "They must have figured out what the Reno set has known for years: there really is nothing better for a good drunk or a bad hangover than a large number eight." He handed her the plastic spoon and wooden chopsticks she'd be needing for her soup.

A waiter he didn't know delivered their spring rolls and refilled their glasses with water. Amy tried to get Matt's attention again, but the waiter came back to drop off the herbs and peppers for their pho.

"You think everything is going to be all right?" she asked Matt once the waiter had left.

"What do you mean?"

"I never thought I would be six months pregnant before I was even married," she said. "I guess I mean, do you think it is all going to be all right?"

"You were four months pregnant before you were even engaged," he said, trying to be funny.

"Matt, I'm serious," she said, her face proving it. "We're doing the right thing, right?"

"What do you mean?"

"I mean, we messed up, but we are trying to make it right, right?"

"Yeah, we're making everything right. Don't worry about it," he said. "It's all going to be fine."

The waiter came out with a large plastic platter and set their soups in front of them and went to the next table without saying a word. "Excuse me," Matt said, getting the man's attention. "Can I get a Hanoi, please?" The man nodded and walked quickly to the big refrigerator by the cash register.

"It's a beer," he said, shortly before the waiter delivered it to their table. "Did I ever tell you the story about the first time I came here?"

"There's a story?" she asked.

"Yeah," he said, taking a large bite of a spring roll and pushing a slice of the beef into the hot broth of his soup. "So it's a couple of years ago. My brother John is working as a valet over there at the Silver Legacy." He pointed out the window across the street with his chopsticks. "John was always going to exotic places to eat, which I always thought was a little annoying, so I was actually a little pissed off when he told me and Charlie to meet him here."

She nodded, smiling, blowing on a spoonful of her broth to cool it down.

"So he tells us to meet him here at noon, and Charlie and I get here about five minutes after. We

look around and the place is packed. I mean *packed.*
They told us it was Tết and they just shrugged.
Every time we'd try to get service, 'It's Tết.' John was
nowhere to be found. You have to remember, this
is like '98 or '99, none of us has cell phones, so we
just wait. I'm looking around and all I can think
of is the movie *Good Morning, Vietnam.* Have you seen
that?"

"No," she said, shaking her head. "Is that a
movie?"

"Is that a movie?" he said, mocking her. "It was
like the only good movie that Robin Williams was
ever in, but that is neither here nor there." He
dropped a piece of uncooked meet into his soup
broth and twirled it around with his chopsticks
while it cooked. "There's this scene where he's at
this market in Vietnam and he's making fun of the
food they are selling at the open market. Anyway,
that's all I can see while we're standing there. Like,
'what has John gotten us into?'"

"But you love this place," she said.

"Yeah, that's what I am saying. That was my first
time here. I love it now, but then all I could see

was all of this raw food and stuff that I hadn't seen before. I was like eighteen. I was an idiot. Anyway, so Charlie and I grab a spot and we are sitting there just shooting the shit," he said, realizing that she wouldn't like that word even before she crinkled her forehead at him. "So we're just chatting, wondering how we got a seat during Tết, wondering where John is, and so on. Then one of the owners or their family members comes over with one of those old, white cordless phones. We're the only white guys in here. She comes up to the table and says, 'Is one of you Charlie?' She said it really loud, too. We were just so embarrassed. So Charlie takes the phone and puts his head down in his hands. He says, 'John, you called a Vietnamese restaurant and asked for Charlie?' I could tell he was waiting for John to respond, but he cut him off, 'You don't see anything wrong with that?'" Matt asked, laughing into his water.

"What's so funny about that?" she asked.

"Seriously?" he asked. "'Charlie' is a slur for Vietnamese people."

"How?"

"Long story," he said. "It's military lingo from the Vietnam War."

"That's lovely," she said.

"That's not the point. The point is, John's that guy who calls a Vietnamese restaurant and asks for Charlie. Even though he knows I am sitting right there, he still asks for Charlie. It was hilarious, and after that we had a great lunch and I've been coming back here ever since."

"Have you always gotten a number eight?"

"It was funny," he said, protesting her desire to move on. "But yes, I love the rare steak pho and the spring rolls. Every time. On a few nights, a few spectacularly drunken nights, I'd get the spring rolls, the number eight, and a number sixty-four, which is a huge rice plate of barbecued pork. It's amazing. You always get the brisket pho?" He knew the answer, but he was tired of talking.

"Yep. When I'd come here to study or work, it was the perfect comfort food. Especially while you were gone." He smiled at her sentiment. It was a sweet statement and he knew she meant it that way. The waiter came by and filled up his glass with water.

"Matt," she said quietly. "My parents won't return any of my phone calls."

"I was wondering about that," he said. "What should we do?"

"That's kind of why I told you," she said. "I know they are embarrassed or ashamed of me or whatever, but I didn't expect them to ignore my phone calls."

"What do you need to tell them?" he asked.

"Nothing, really," she said. "I mean, we are going to have a baby in a few months and we have planning for the wedding to do. But I guess they don't want to be a part of any of it."

"I knew they were tough, but I didn't expect them to do that," he said. He grabbed a thin slice of meat off of the plate next to him with his chopsticks, swirling it around in the broth. The meat was rubbery when he put it in his mouth. The soup was beginning to cool down now; not hot enough to cook the meat all the way through. He spun some rice noodles and a jalapeño slice onto the plastic spoon and poured it into his mouth, chewing it for as long as he could before the spice made him swallow. He threw his head back and drank half of his Hanoi beer in one swallow, attempting to extinguish the mixture of everything he had just eaten.

"Oh my God," he said looking down at his beer, still up at his lips.

"What is it?" Amy asked, starting to turn to see what he was looking at.

"Don't look," he said quietly into his beer, his eyes cutting over her shoulder.

"What is it? What are you looking at?" she asked.

"Did you see a tall guy with two girls walk in a few minutes ago?" he asked.

"No, when did they come in?"

"I don't know. Must've been just now though. I just noticed them."

"What is it?"

"He's tall, like six foot six, well built. He's wearing aviator sunglasses, an olive green tee shirt, cargo pants, and something like hiking boots. He has a huge watch on his wrist, too. He looks like he's about sixty or so, but in good shape. He's still got a military haircut. Not like a ridiculous high and tight, but still clean," Matt said, still holding his glass to his mouth and staring at the man he was describing, ready to avert his eyes at any second. "He's sitting there with two young girls. They are totally hookers—wearing the whole hooker outfit: fishnets, short skirts, too much makeup. Geez," he added, before looking back at Amy.

"So?" Amy asked.

"It's this whole scene. It's the way he's talking to them, really low tones. He's leaning in and whispering, doing all of the talking and they are doing the listening. They look all scared, like they couldn't be sitting closer together. It's just weird."

"I guess I don't get it," she said.

"It's just weird," he said again. "He's clean, he's well kept. And they are obviously streetwalkers."

"I mean," she said, obviously trying to move the conversation forward, "this is Reno. We're on Fifth Street. There are whores."

"That's not it," he said, still staring at them over her shoulder. "He's sitting in a Vietnamese restaurant with two girls who are obviously whores and they look terrified, like he's explaining some fantasy from his days in Nam. God, look at how he's talking to them," he muttered over the mouth of his beer bottle.

"It still doesn't make sense," she said.

"Did you just say, 'this is Reno, there are whores'?" he asked her, breaking his stare from the three seated over Amy's shoulder.

"Yeah, I mean, this is Reno. It's kind of famous for whores, isn't it?"

"That's so weird," he said, smiling at her.

"Why? Because I said that? I am not saying it's okay, I'm just saying that it is."

"No, because that's exactly what Charlie said to me on Saturday."

"Why were you talking about whores with Charlie?"

"He needed me to go to the post office for him and pick up something. It was the old post office down on Lake or Virginia Street or whatever, the one in the great old building. I went in there and I was staring at the ceiling and the walls. The tables are old art deco things, and there are swastikas all around them. It was strange. So I am staring at the ceilings and the walls and the tables as I am walking

out of there, not really paying attention to anything, and as my eyes are coming down I make eye
contact with this girl. She's like thirty or so, kind
of cute and innocent looking, not dressed unusu-
ally or anything like that. But as soon as we make
eye contact, she gets this little smirk on her face and
she drops her eyes to my crotch and then back up to
my eyes."

"Really?" she asked.

"Yeah, so I break eye contact with her and I get
ten steps past her before I put it together. Why is she
standing at a table in a downtown post office and
staring people down? Why did she smirk and look
at my crotch? Then later, I am driving south on
Arlington, right in front of the Sands. It's like one in
the morning. I start to accelerate past Second Street,
not really paying attention to anything, when I see
this girl there. She's youngish, blonde, wearing very
little, so I stare at her, sort of absentmindedly. She
stares back, and actually turns all the way around as I
drive by so that she can stare at me. So I asked Charlie about it all. And he says what you said: 'This is
Reno, there are whores.' And it made sense."

"You grew up here, though," she said.

"Yeah, I guess I knew about it, I'd heard of all of those places, but I didn't know about it downtown. I mean, just a block south of here."

"I guess I am just surprised that you are surprised," she said.

He put all of the raw slices of meat left on the little plate into his soup, hoping that there was still enough heat to cook it all of the way through. Stirring it with his chopsticks, he squeezed in a little hot sauce and stirred it again.

"I'm sorry," he said. "It's just how I eat it."

"I don't care how you eat your soup, Matt," she said, not breaking her gaze this time. "I couldn't care less about that. I don't care about whores or whatever else you want to avoid me with, either. I care about how we're going to make it. I care about what we are going to do now that you are home. I care about our lives. And I can't seem to figure out if you care at all."

"Everything is going to be fine," he said smiling, grabbing both of her hands in his.

"Matt," she said, not willing to being brushed off

again. "I am twenty-four weeks pregnant. We are going to get married in a month. Then we are going to have a baby. And I can't even get my parents to return my phone calls. Can you please, please tell me how in the hell everything's going to be fine?" Her voice was still soft, but it wasn't calm, and she was crying gently.

"We've been through worse," he said, still trying to smile.

"*You've* been through worse, Matt," she said, raising her voice only slightly.

Her words stung, but they were true. He had been through worse, but before she met him one night, her world was church and college and her parents.

"Look, Amy," he said quietly but forcefully enough to get her attention. "The guys in this picture," he said, holding up the picture of himself and his brothers camping. "They don't exist anymore. None of them do. This is it," he said, putting the picture down and holding up the picture of their unborn child. "This is all we have that matters anymore. You and me and this. Your parents can disown us. It doesn't matter. It's you, me, and this little guy. That's it."

The owner came back over to the table to refill their water glasses and take their plates. He didn't acknowledge that Amy was crying or that they were obviously in a personal discussion. He just took their plates and walked away without his usual questions about the quality of the food and the service.

"We aren't going to let something like this kill us. We're getting married. We're having a baby. Your parents can make up their minds on whether or not they are going to show us the love they have always preached. Who knows, tomorrow might be colder or it might be warmer. A year from now we might be staring down another crisis. And twenty years from now we'll be coming here, still eating a number eight and a number twelve, and laughing at all of the little things that we never thought we would be able to handle." He paused, squeezing her hands tighter.

"Are you with me?" he asked.

She nodded.

"Then everything is going to be just fine."

About the Author

CALEB S. CAGE is a graduate of the US Military Academy, West Point, and a veteran of the Iraq War. He is the coauthor of the book *The Gods of Diyala: Transfer of Command in Iraq* (Texas A&M University Press, 2008), about his time as a platoon leader. His essays and fiction have appeared in *War, Literature & the Arts, Red Rock Review, High Country News, Small Wars Journal,* and various other publications and anthologies.